Soweto Stories

Miriam Tlali was born in Doornfontein in Johannesburg and grew up in Sophiatown. She enrolled as a BA student at the University of the Witwatersrand just before blacks were barred from entering the university and studied African Administration, Psychology, Sociology, History of Art, Zoology and African Languages. She now lives and writes in Soweto. Her novel *Amandla!* was banned in South Africa within six weeks of its publication in 1980. This ban has recently been lifted. Her first novel, *Muriel at the Metropolitan*, has recently been reissued in Longmans' African Classics Series.

Soweto

Stories

Miriam Tlali

WITH AN INTRODUCTION BY
LAURETTA NGCOBO

PANDORA PRESS
London Sydney Wellington

First published by Pandora Press, an imprint of the Trade Division of Unwin Hyman, in 1989.

© Miriam Tlali 1989
'The Point of No Return' was first published in
Staffrider in 1977.

PANDORA PRESS
Unwin Hyman Limited
15/17 Broadwick Street
London W1V 1FP

Unwin Hyman Inc
8 Winchester Place, Winchester, MA 01890

Allen & Unwin Australia Pty Ltd
P.O. Box 764, 8 Napier Street, North Sydney,
NSW 2060

Allen & Unwin NZ Ltd (in association with the Port Nicholson Press)
60 Cambridge Terrace, Wellington, New Zealand

To be published in South Africa by David Philip Publisher Ltd under the title Footsteps in the Quag: Stories and Dialogues From Soweto

British Library Cataloguing in Publicatin Data

Tlali, Miriam
    Soweto stories.
    I. Title
    823[F]

ISBN 0 04 440350X

Printed in Great Britain by Cox & Wyman Ltd, Reading

This book is dedicated to

Lida, Derelies, Tania, Patty and Marjan

the courageous Dutch women

for having made it possible – just this once –
for me to write without a care in the world, and
with no tears in my eyes

and

to Mineke

for having remembered

Contents

Introduction by Lauretta Ngcobo   ix

Vigil with the Flies and the Bed bugs   1

Mm'a-Lithoto   12

'Fud-u-u-a!'   27

Dimomona   43

'Go In Peace, Tobias Son of Opperman'   66

Metamorphosis   78

Gone Are Those Days   93

Devil at a Dead end   102

The Point of No Return   119

'Masechaba's Erring 'Child'   138

Introduction

A South African woman writer in the 1980s is a rare find. As such Miriam Tlali joins that small but significant band of women who have been recording the experiences and the collective responses of our society to all the changes, challenges and cultural traumas of the past few centuries in South Africa. In order for us to accord her a rightful place in this order of literary figures and to get the correct perspective of her message we need to look very briefly at the history of that writing.

South African black scripted literature is about one hundred and fifty years old if we date it from Ntsikana's first written poetry composition written in the 1820s. Right from the start the African literary experience was fraught with difficulties. Acquiring literacy from the missionaries was both a help and a hindrance. At first the Africans wrote books and articles for magazines but they were expected to portray work with a religious content. Most of the books were of an educational nature. This was what the missionaries expected of them and when they directed their efforts towards social and political aspects as they saw them, conflict inevitably developed. Some of these attitudes have continued to this day affecting many writers who depend on the missionary presses for publication. There are innumerable accounts of religious censorship in the past that are not based on the quality of writing but on the choice of views and themes expressed. Great as the Christian contribution has been to African development, it is hard to understand why the Christian outlook has often sought to destroy the inner core of African thought, belief and feeling about life's changes as well as the basic philosophy of that life. It has been hard for the African to understand why the African way of life is deemed incompatible with a Christian way of life. In spite of these early handicaps African writing has thrived for more than a century, responding vigorously to the traumatic changes that Africans faced in those days.

Most of the early writing was concerned with preserving a culture that was severely under attack, indicating a deep loyalty to African beliefs, customs, traditions and oral literature. Later in the century, people like Tiyo Soga ventured slowly into the Western type of literature, translating books such as John Bunyan's *The Pilgrim's Progress*. Others, like Gqoba, at about the same time, wrote about the encroaching problems brought on by education and Christianity, two potent forces at the time. Most of Gqoba's writings based on acculturation were published after his death by another writer, Walter Rubusana, in his book *Zemk' Inkomo Magwala Ndini* in which he bewailed the loss of self-identity amongst the African people. There are many writers at the close of the century who wrote profusely on the effects of migratory labour and the destruction of social life under the hammer of industrialisation. A careful examination of the literary development in South Africa shows a close alignment between

the escalation of the political situation under the Colon-
ists and certain remarkable changes in our literature. In
the turbulence of our history this is a literary act of
significance.

About the turn of the century we see the emergence
of people like Mqhayi who began to write imaginatively.
His novel *Ityala La Mawele* (1914) is particularly
significant. In this story, which is a dispute of inherit-
ance, Mqhayi reveals African judicial law and
procedures. It was during this wrestling period, when
the danger to our culture and traditions was no longer
in doubt, that many writers directed their efforts at
reinstating the validity of life as they had known it.
They wrote historical prose fiction to give the nation a
sense of pride and identity. Thomas Mofolo's classic
novel *Chaka*, based on Shaka the great king of the
Zulus, belongs to this period. More and more novels
appeared dealing with the devastating industrial experience and its twin sister, migratory labour. The books
show a puzzled ʾeducated class who had adhered to
Christian teachings but could see themselves set on the
road to failure. They reflect bewilderment. These
writers were faced with the paradox of creating or
fashioning a new indigenous character, while the
dynamics of the situation pointed to the destruction of
the culture in which that character had to be rooted and
flourish.

This was a vibrant growing literature until about the
1920s when there was a sudden trailing off, a loss of
energy somewhere in the pit of society which was at
first imperceptible. Another look at the political scene
shows that this coincided with the creation of the Union
of South Africa when Great Britain handed over the
country and all political power to the white people of
South Africa and to the exclusion of the African people.

With the loss of the land, the Africans' most prized and valuable possession, came their confinement to the worst areas of the country, so small that they and their stock were on the verge of starvation. The deputations and the delegations that they sent in succession to both the South African rulers and the British ex-rulers were falling on deaf ears. This had an insidious effect on the African personality. The period reflects a deep-seated self-doubt at the core of African life. The awareness of loss and isolation in the African spirit is revealed in the long years of silence that followed on the literary front. It is as though all African expression was muzzled. Psychologically this is not difficult to understand. The period marks the Africans' first awareness of themselves as an oppressed people. Our politicians spent years making fruitless representations, trying to convince the white man that they were reasonable and capable not only of adjusting to the white man's ways but also of negotiating issues amicably for all concerned. They did everything they could to polish the image and fit the part. It is therefore not surprising that very little of any literary merit was written. It is also worthy of note that what was written tended to emulate Western styles of writing. Vilakazi experimented with Zulu poetry in verse, rhyme and metre – a totally alien style, and Dhomo wrote his epic poem *The Valley of a Thousand Hills* in impeccable English – a truly Westernised poem. These were years of appeasement. The period lasted until the Nationalists came to power in the late 1940s. The Afrikaner does not believe in soothing and massaging the wounds of history. Their abrasive approach was clearly spelt out in many ways.

During the 1950s we entered a period of political confrontation with the oppressor. It started with the defiance campaign of 1952. The decade ended with the escalation of that confrontation, marked by the pan-Africanist-led events of 1960 – the most memorable of which was the massacre of demonstrators in Sharpeville. This political confrontation gave birth to a new type of literature, a literature that reflected the traumatic times and the end of futile efforts to convince white people of our good intentions. At this time we fought to convince ourselves of our worthiness. We no longer cared what the oppressor thought. We rejected the distorted image and developed a new assertion of our blackness, our dignity and worthiness on black terms. The government reacted with predictable violence. They were determined to squash the spirit of assertion as it reared its head. Not only were the politicians hounded, but our writers too. Many of their books were confiscated. In their reports of the 'self-mutilating ghettos' the journalists exposed what the system was doing to men, women and the fabric of society as a whole. Writers like Henry Nxumalo hit more forcibly at the government when they exposed the truth about the terror in the prisons and the cruel, inhumane conditions found in the convict labour system. Nxumalo, it is believed, paid for this with his life by his mysterious death.

Many of our writers of that period were forced into exile by the unbearable pressures that were put on writers as a class as well as the banning of their works. Many have been able to write in exile but their books are still not acceptable in South Africa. The resurgence of a black spirit ushered in by these writers has marked the beginning of a new type of writing – protest writing. Powerful writers such as Alex La Guma, Can Themba, Ezekiel Mphahlele and Henry Nxumalo spoke for the oppressed. Bessie Head was also a product of this period. She was forced out of the country and could only find her full expression in exile in Botswana. For a long time the government almost succeeded in eliminating not only the spirit, but the writers as well. Once more the literary field was left bereft of all means of expression – mute and dumb. Then came the 1960 Sharpeville massacre. The shock of it, the arrests, bannings and the general intimidation of the whole society left the people stunned, but with no-one to articulate the Africans' underlying thoughts and feelings. A long silence lasted throughout the 1960's and the early 1970s. But there was a qualitative difference in this silence to the earlier muteness of submission. People were silenced but not dispirited. It was no longer subservience that silenced them. A new spirit of reorientation had the effect of energising people.

At the beginning of the 1970s a new spirit emerged with dramatic force. The youth of South Africa discovered a less vulnerable form of protest writing – a new form of poetry. For reasons that are hard to explain the poets and their writing enjoyed a form of official tolerance not accorded to any other kind of writer. This poetry became the only outlet for the increasingly grim experience of the 1960s and 1970s. For the first time literary expression in our writing took on a completely political perspective. Social problems were of far less concern to writers. Protest writing had arrived, to the virtual exclusion of anything else that might engage the literary mind. Harsh experience 'drove creativity back to itself and forced it to be its own hiding place' in the words of Nadine Gordimer. These were street corner poets who pursued neither fame nor aesthetics. Instead they sought to affirm black identity and to reject unequivocally the white man's right to legislate against their dignity and their self-determination. With this in mind one poet wrote:

To label my utterings poetry
And myself a poet
Would be as self-deluding
As the planners of Parallel Development.
I recall the anguish of the persecuted
Whose words and whimpers of woe
Wrung from them by bestial laws.
They stand one chained band
Silently asking one of the other
'Will it never be the fire next time?'

This period of poetic licence radiated a warmth that slowly thawed the climate of writing throughout the country. A few writers slowly emerged again and the novel made its slow resurgence on the scene. Among the writers in this reawakening stands Miriam Tlali – a woman. She dared hold and express opinions. She dared not only to speak out against the South African system, but also against the dominance of male writing which had attended black literature from the very beginning. She struck out bold and fearless. She could not help but be noticed for she was not only among the first novelists to resurface, but she was also the first woman novelist inside South Africa to take her place among the national gallery of our black literary figures. She has kept her place and grown from the 1970s to record the history of the burning 1980s. She is among the very few writers who have refused to be intimidated and 'smoked' out of South Africa, by the harsh treatment that is reserved for black writers. She writes from the heart of those turbulent cities. Not only does she write herself, but she is also, together with a few others, involved in the mammoth task of coaxing and training new writers for our people. At the time of writing we are beginning to see the fruits of their work, for a few young writers are beginning to appear in recent short story anthologies such as *From the Heart – Women in South Africa* edited by Siriti Sa Sechaba and *Sometimes When It Rains* edited by Ann Oosthuizen.

In a paradoxical way the interests of black city people sometimes stand diametrically opposed to those of rural people; one half the antithesis of the other. We all suffer the same oppression but we perceive it differently. The sabre of white apartheid rule cuts divisions even among people of one race. There are instances where the government legislates differently for city people as against rural people, as with the Bantu Authorities Act and the Urban Areas Act. And where rural life reflects a certain degree of stability founded on tradition and a pride in all things African, city lifestyles impose a certain fragmentation with regard to African social values. In a country with such divisions we see Tlali as a city writer, contemplating city contradictions and looking for possible solutions.

Her first book, *Muriel at the Metropolitan,* explores with aching empathy the problems of the poor city blacks who live in the heart of affluence but must endure utter poverty. The goods in the shops so tantalisingly displayed are beyond the means of many. They then resort to the 'never-never' schemes of credit buying. Muriel works in such a shop whose clientele is entirely African, a flourishing shop founded on their inevitable failure to meet their commitments. Muriel ponders her own compromised position as she issues them with documents of repossession, putting a seal to their final despair in a system that was never intended to benefit them. From the vantage point of the shop's office clerk, she looks at the vicious economic spiral bearing down on vulnerable customers. No matter how deep the social and political divisions may go white economic interests depend on the Africans' vast economic power. No matter how meagre the individual's earnings, the Africans' collective buying power is lucrative. We form a large pool of labour around cities. Cities and the white business community benefit from black labour. This system ensures that our communities remain permanently on or below the poverty line for we do not benefit from our earning power.

Tlali's second book, *Amandla!*, reflects a very different historical reality of our cities. The book records the political turbulence that set in with the pupils' uprising of 1976. The book portrays the start of the troubles that we witness today in the streets of South Africa's cities. It records the violence of the white system against an unarmed population of very young and very angry people. She points to the wide divisions that became apparent overnight between the young and the old, divisions which have in some cases widened and created strange differences of opinions between parents and their children. In its effort to capture the vision of the burning communities and record the diary of events it presents such a wide canvas that it almost lacks focus.

In this latest volume of short stories Tlali strikes out in a very different tone of voice, plaintive and meditative. She speculates and offers possible explanations as to why city life is so sad. In this volume she turns her eyes on to her own community, focussing self-consciously for the African eyes only – on the wounds sustained in the collapse of our societies. Her eye lingers long and hard on the lives of women in particular. It is as though she has taken a step back to watch the devastation all around. There is an anguished note in most of these stories as she examines working conditions, marriage problems, poverty and poor housing, drinking problems, male fickleness and general degeneration. With her feet deeply planted in the city, her eyes look back on the last warp of tradition, hankering after a lost way of life. She indicates that city problems are due to the loss of traditions and peoples rootlessness.

In her story MMA LITHOTO this longing is at its strongest. She extols the virtues of the extended family. In it, she maintains, 'you know who to "run to". It is important for you to know that you are not alone, that you are never an "orphan". There is always someone in the "family" who is under obligation to "stand" by you.' Tlali is more aware than many present day city writers of the cultural loss suffered as a result of the city experience. Looking at society in transition on the context of the family, she perceives tradition as the only 'salvation' for the African people. Only if Keletso and Thabo go back to their cultural roots can they be saved. Otherwise they are like driftwood 'Ba thefuloa ke lifefo tsa bophelo' (beings blown about by the storms of life). 'No-one can succeed to destroy us if we know ourselves the "laws" that our ancestors have left with us'.

In the same story and in several others she views the fractured family structure and how women are generally disadvantaged. Many women have had to take on the role of maintaining their families single handed, where the men have abdicated their responsiblities and taken to drink or fallen victim to other vices and the law. Girls prove more supportive of their parents and have in many cases taken over the role traditionally occupied by their male counterparts – that of supporting their aged parents. When men in the West 'walk out' they pack their cases, call a taxi and catch a train, out and away they go, leaving their wife and children distressed but protected and secure in the family home. Whereas in South Africa, when such times come it is often the woman who has to 'walk out', often with her children trailing behind her. She leaves her husband comfortable and secure in his home. African women have no homes as such; its always a mans home and his peoples home. All this within the context of the city, where one little home is shared by three of four generations. This alone is a major factor in the break up of many homes. Her stories are suffused with a feeling of spacelessness, a feeling of nowhere-to-turn-to. On this point Tlali is not on the side of tradition, for customary practice supports the view that the family home belongs to the man and his people. Now and again such conflicts of view arise in Tlalis' stories, revealing a society at the crossroads. This clash with tradition is further enhanced in *Masechabas Erring Child*.

Masechaba not only tolerates her husbands infidelity, she appears to even encourage it. She pays the price for her security as a wife. Through her protagonist Tholoana, Tlali questions this attitude. The whole tone of the story is that of disapproval. She sees the complicity as a betrayal of woman; something that only a woman in despair would give in to. Seeing that this form of subjection and complicity is rooted in and sanctioned by tradition and is a remnant of polygamy, one can be forgiven in thinking that Tlali might be comfortable with this. But this is not so. This inconsistancy with tradition is a feature found in the whole of society, a wavering society with conflicting attitudes and altering values. It is a time of acceptance and rejection. Nothing is wholly one or the other and society is divided at the core.

Behind the facade of a lively, robust, fighting fit society, walking the streets of many cities is the slow death that Tlali deplores. Through her roving eye we see beneath the skin of dominant men, we see how weak they really are; how decadent and incapacitated. Without any direct reference to the government and its aparteid system, she shows us how deeply the cancerous policies have eaten into our way of life. But above everything, Tlali is searching for an antidote, looking into her past for some prescription handed down from the dim past that could sustain us until freedom comes.

Lauretta Ngcobo 1988

Vigil with the Flies and the Bed Bugs

It all happened because I missed the bus to Mekho-khong, a village in the remote area near Roma Valley of the Matsieng District, Lesotho. Someone should have warned me that when a Mosotho says 'Khubelu' he does not necessarily mean 'red' in the strict sense of the word but that any shade on either side of the spectrum could be applicable. If it had not been for my careless assumption and complacency, I would not have spent those horrific hours in a small room in Maseru, at the mercy of whizzing, agonising flies and that army of blood-thirsty bed bugs.

I had arrived too early at the Maseru bus terminus, I was informed by a man when I asked whether the bus to Matsieng had arrived. The kind smiling local resident had put my mind at rest. He said, 'You just sit some-where and watch the "Makoloi" as they drive in. The Mekhokhong bus is easy to recognise. She's a red-coloured beauty and you'll have no difficulty identifying her.'

I was happy and contented. The prospect of a quiet recline with a book under the shade of some trees a few metres away was pleasant indeed. I have often wondered whether I should blame that night on my insatiable desire to be left alone to read. I had been reading *Giovanni's Room* by James Baldwin and I could not wait to resume the absorbing story. I would cast an occasional glance at the dusty gravel road from the Leriba District to see if the 'red beauty' had arrived.

Scores of buses with colourful, bold and attractive names converged and departed from a spacious dusty concourse. If it had not been for my complete absorption in *Giovanni's Room*, the continuous loud roaring of engines and the whistling, singing, chatting, bustling multitudes of commuters would have been unbearable.

I glanced occasionally at the wide square where the buses circled, taking their places in turns, coming to a standstill at their allotted positions. It was not easy to ignore what was happening. The touts howled loudly, competing with one another for business. Passengers dodged and scampered around in confusion, not certain which way to go.

'Wait, wait, Ntate! Please!' one shouted, annoyed at the touts' impatience.

'Where are you going to? Tyafyaneng, Peka, Leribe? Come, Ntate, I'll take your luggage!'

'Who said I was going to TY, Kapa Peka, or Leribe? Please leave my luggage, Ntate.'

And so it went on . . . passengers arguing with touts, some smiling through it all . . . trying to take it philosophically . . . others really getting furious at the unwelcome intrusion. It was all in the way of business, so the touts took it. They had to survive. The more customers you brought to a bus owner, the more commission you got, so the children could eat . . . 'Bane ba Haja.'

Hundreds of passengers swarmed around the entrances to buses like a cluster of bees. First come, first seated. If you did not rush for a place to 'put a buttock' you would stand for miles and miles. Everyone who passed through the narrow passage would rub against you and you would sway from one side to the other as the bus meandered along the mountainous route, penetrating the untamed countryside. At the entrance it was everyone for his or her self and 'God for us all'.

'Ao! Ichi! . . . Be-Butle hle Ntate! Jonna! Ba mpshatlile mokottana peop! Jonna Ka le Bona..a..a!' 'Someone has crushed my testicles, my seed pocket.' It was a timely joke and everyone looked in the direction of the distressed sufferer.

'Just stop your language, there are children with us,' a woman's voice called from the cluster. It was not easy to see her. She was buried beneath colourful blankets. Men whistled as they flapped the blankets over their shoulders and pushed their way in. Business was good. The touts stood to one side and watched, urging the passengers on with spontaneous poetry – 'A li roka, moshanyana.'

The names painted on the sides of the buses in beautiful, stylish letters were themselves an attraction. You felt proud to be a passenger and that meant business.

'Kalamazoo.'

'Thabang Baheso' (rejoice my fellow men).

'Lebohang Matabele' (say thanks to the Matabele).

'Halala se-ea-le-moea' (hail to you the flying one).

'Tsotang Bafokeng' (express your pride, Bafokeng).

'Le ha re le Boneng' (what will you say you have beheld)?

'Eea lslesel' (it speeds along proudly).

'Ha ho pohopeli' (I am the boss).

I read the names until my eyes ached from the red

dust. Scores and scores of buses zoomed into the concourse. Some made a complete circle like parading models and the women ululated, removing their bright headcloths as they surged forward to 'greet' the colourful beauties.

It was business. Even the smiling vendors carrying their wares carefully on their heads drew nearer to the buses in order to display them. It was business, it was life. The children would eat.

The hours went by and there was still no sign of the 'red beauty'. When the shadows of the trees became longer and the sun seemed only a short distance away from the horizon on the west I grew less and less preoccupied by my reading. How could the vehicle take so long to arrive? I feared that something must have gone wrong. Could it be that the bus only travelled on some and not all weekdays, I wondered? Perhaps my adviser had not been so well informed after all.

I stood up and approached a group of men standing near a yellow bus. 'When is the bus to Mekhokhong arriving, Ntate?' I asked one of them. He looked at his companions and pondered a while before he checked the time on his watch.

'But the bus came in nearly two hours ago, Morena.'

One of the men nodded and said, 'It went long ago. How long have you been here, Ntate?'

My heart sank. 'Since midday,' I replied with a slightly shaky voice. 'Someone told me to look out for a red bus.'

I had seen an orange bus, a purplish one, a pinkish one and a yellow one. These were the only colours near red that I had seen arrive. I was certain that I had not seen a single red bus. I tried to explain to them, showing the colours I had seen by pointing to their ties, women's hats and dresses. Colours such as purple, rust and pink were difficult to describe as the Sotho language had no equivalent. They seemed puzzled but eager to help me.

'You say you saw a bus with the redness of an orange, Sir?' one said.

I nodded, feeling hopeless.

'Then that's the one you should have got on to, Ntate! I'm afraid that you'll have to wait until tomorrow for another one. There's no other bus to Mekhokhong, Ntate.'

And with that the men seemed eager to get rid of me and continued with their more urgent conversation, ignoring me totally.

I moved away slowly. The sun had sunk and left an orange glow where the sky met with the undulating line of the Maloti mountains. I had travelled from my home village of Tsikoana early that morning, knowing that I would be in Matsieng before sunset of the same day. But I was now stranded in the unfamiliar town of Maseru. Where would I sleep? I had heard many stories of how people had been robbed and cheated in Maseru, particularly unknown travellers, and I had observed during the brief periods that I had been there how most of the Basotho could change from being tolerant and accommodating hosts to hard and inhospitable in a flash. It had saddened me and I longed for the days of my youth when a traveller could walk into any home along the way at night, be welcomed and be sure of enjoying a restful night. Those days were now a thing of the past. I moved into the darkness and the uncertainty of what lay ahead.

I walked along a street and a man followed in the same direction. He greeted me amicably and his friendly manner made me feel immediately well disposed towards him. At least the Basotho custom of establishing a familiar and spontaneous friendship between complete strangers had not been removed from them. It had withstood the corrupting foreign ways of rigid, cold aloofness. There was still some hope for humanity, I thought, as we moved along the street together. I felt that I could trust him. I informed him of my sad predicament. I *had* to find a place where I could spend the night. I did manage to make him understand that I had no intention of imposing myself on anyone. In the progressively impersonal atmosphere typical of all towns one had to conform. It was simply imperative that one learnt to adapt to the 'foreign' practice of 'buying one's way out' at all times.

'I am willing to pay a reasonable fee for any "safe accommodation" and would be grateful if you could assist me in finding such a place. I am a complete stranger, Ntate.'

He was a resident of Maseru, he told me, and he would certainly help. He set my mind at ease by adding, 'There are many places here in Maseru where you can find a place to sleep. There are many hotels.'

I felt confident that everything was going to be all right and that I had no reason to be anxious any more. He spoke of a number of small hotels. Just a block away, he said, was a place owned by a widow named Mmamohau (mother of mercy) because of her tender and kind attitude towards travellers. She made a living by letting rooms in her large cottage, he explained, as all of her children had married and gone to live on their own and she no longer needed to occupy the whole house. There were always vacant rooms available my 'friend' said. It seemed that I had been extremely fortunate to meet this man.

After introducing me to the charitable woman the man left. I followed her to the room I would spend the night in. She pointed to the bed covered with a clean white counterpane, disturbing myriads of flies which seemed to be everywhere as she moved her arm. She pointed, smiling proudly.

'You can rest there, my son. You must be tired after all the trouble you have had. Have a good night's sleep, my son.'

Mmamohau then disappeared into the long passage, shutting the door behind her.

It was in the middle of the month of December. The room was hot with stagnant air, and flies . . . numerous buzzing flies that settled on the walls, the table, the bed, everywhere. It suddenly struck me that the kind lady had not been at all bothered by these insects, that she made no effort to brush them off her face as she spoke.

I removed my coat and hooked it on a peg against one wall. The wooden floor creaked as I walked across it and stopped next to the only window in the room. Allowing some air to circulate in the room would certainly remove some of the stifling hot atmosphere. One could even persuade some of the many flies to leave the apartment by fanning them towards the open window. I was not going to treat these pests with the tenderness of my landlady! The wooden shutter over the old French window would just not yield to my pressure. It seemed to have been securely nailed. I gave up trying and dropped heavily on to the infested counterpane, to the annoyance of the insects which flew off in all directions.

'Sleep is an enemy,' the Basotho say.

I must have been asleep for nearly an hour because the clock had just struck three times. There was now only about an hour and a half to go before the cracks in the old wooden ceiling would show some light from the sky above, I consoled myself as I rubbed my burning eyes. I had never waited for the break of day like this in all my life. I had gone through hell.

In my desperate attempt to escape from stinging buzzing flies I had crawled into the neat bed with clean white sheets. I had thought that if I kept my head under the sheets all night that would save me from the flies. I would just have to live through the ordeal of suffocation, taking occasional peeps out of the covers for breath. But that was like jumping from the frying pan into the fire. Hungry bed bugs started invading. Exactly half an hour after the landlady had wished me a 'good' night's sleep, I had switched off the light hoping for some rest. They must have converged on me immediately, for as soon as I moved my hand to scratch the first itchy spot, the unmistakable smell of a crushed bed bug became apparent. Then my whole body started itching and I did not have enough fingers with which to scratch.

In the end I abandoned the bed and decided to spread the blanket on the floor. The abominable creatures must have smelt me out because they followed me there. I felt sure that they must have been oozing from the wooden slats below. I knelt on the blanket and crouched over, trying to nap, but it was no good. I spent the night fanning away flies and crushing bed bugs with the heel of one of my shoes. I tried to run away from the floor by sitting on the chair next to the table. I dozed like a nurse on night duty. I looked at the blood-stained pillow case and sheets on the 'clean' bed. The flies had begun to swarm on the red spots, possibly to suck what remained of the bed bugs. Perhaps my hostess had spread these white sheets on the bed in the hope that the loathsome insects would behave themselves. But household pests have no moral codes of behaviour.

They followed me everywhere. I felt certain that David's torment and contemplated escape from his misery in *Giovanni's Room* could never match mine.

Sleep is an enemy. How very true that saying is. All the senses in my body demanded rest. It became more and more difficult for me to keep my eyes open. I blinked and blinked, afraid to shut my eyes in case the flies smothered my face. I kept yawning and yawning, but I had to be careful not to open my mouth too wide. The thought of whole fat flies settling on my tongue and throat was nauseating to say the least. In order to yawn successfully I cupped my hand over my mouth and could feel the muscles of my jaws crackle from continual distortion. What agony!

Oh sleep, dear sleep – you are a free God-given form of relaxation yet I cannot partake of you, I sat there thinking in self-pity. Was the clock on the wall part of the torture Mmamohau used to punish her inmates? And if so, why? Why would this smiling widow wish to torment others? And if she felt at home with the flies and the bed bugs, why had people never complained to her about them? I was puzzled.

It was only two o'clock in the morning. I shook my head in disgust. I had endured too much. I *had* to think of something to do in order to sleep for a few minutes at least, I said to myself, thinking bitterly of the money I had paid. Such 'hotels' ought to be closed down, or the owners should be forced by law to fumigate their premises. I could not forgive the smiling Mmamohau for having extended her hospitality to me whilst at the same time leaving me at the mercy of the bed bugs and the flies. I should have abandoned my all-enduring modesty and gone straight to her bedroom to lodge my complaint. Even that was pointless, I argued with myself. What would I achieve by that? She would at best give me my money back and wish me luck. I would then be in the streets at the mercy of prowling, barking dogs. I had seen countless emaciated stray dogs roaming through Maseru from one rubbish heap to another.

The British, they built these structures which have now been taken over by the struggling Basotho. When they left (ostensibly giving the Basotho self-rule) these places became breeding places for all sorts of household pests . . . rats, termites and crawling insects of every description.

It occurred to me that I could use the table as a bed. Why had I not thought of it before? Bed bugs do not normally hibernate inside the cracks of tables do they? I had never heard anybody complain about tables being infested with bed bugs. I climbed on to the table. The hard shiny surface felt like stone beneath me. I stretched myself out with my face towards the ceiling where some of the flies had now settled. It was like being crucified. But my body needed the rest.

I must have dropped off, for when the clock chimed three times I started uneasily. I had been sleeping for a whole hour. What an achievement! My sleepy eyes searched for cracks of light in the walls and ceiling announcing the approach of daylight. There were no cracks of light visible. It was a long time before daybreak, a whole hour and a half.

I yawned with my mouth shut. There was still a lingering smell of the bed bugs I had crushed, which made me feel sick. I would have to scrub my hands with soap and lots of water to get rid of it. 'Shit!' I cursed, and spat into the air. 'Why do I keep raising my hands towards my nostrils when I know that I will not be able to bear the stink?'

When you are a really lucky bastard, a good-for-nothing wreck who should be thrown into the wolves' mouths but keeps escaping, the Basotho say that the cursed fellow is as fortunate as a bed bug because in spite of the fact that you know full well what to expect when you crush the damn thing and raise your hand to your nose, you still go ahead and do it!

I turned and slept on my belly, resting my throbbing forehead on my forearms. I wished that I could just let go and sob like a baby. Perhaps then some of the tension and humiliation of having been misled by a hotel tout would ease. It was business all the way.

'Se sa feleng se a Hlola' (that which does not come to an end is an enigma) as we say. My misery came to an end when the cracks in the ceiling and the windows became visible as the early rays of a sun that was still beyond the Matoti mountains came into the room. I rushed out, deliberately breaking the rule that 'motho o a lumelisa ha a tsamaya' (one usually says goodbye to those he leaves behind). The clock struck five times as I left. This time I would not miss the bus with the colour of the redness of an orange.

Mm'a – Lithoto

Paballo sat on the hard bench in Park Station, Johannesburg railway concourse and thought regretfully of her marriage. She did not know whether to stay out of Musi's life for ever. At that moment, she wished she could bid him and his people goodbye and face her future alone.

She looked once more at the bundles of clothing which lay in front of her and wondered whether her once-blissful marriage had been irretrievably lost. Her feelings were shreds of unrelated emotional impulses. One moment she felt like crying at the top of her voice, and seconds later she knew that she did not care. She told herself that in the midst of all the traffic she had at last found peace of mind. That she had finally managed to tear herself away from the unhappy circumstances which made up her married life was an accomplishment she would never regret. Yet at the same time, the pain of estrangement stabbed at her heart, especially when she looked into the innocent unsuspecting face of her three-year-old son, Mzwandile.

Paballo's teenage niece – Mahali – sat next to her, looking at the passing commuters and commenting on the latest fashions girls of her age were wearing. She had rattled on incessantly, trying her best to wrest the attention of her aunt away from the sordid experience they had both been through. They had had to grab clothes, wrap them up into 'lithoto' (bundles) and leave her aunt's home unceremoniously. Where would it all end, she wondered? All she knew was that she would follow her long-suffering aunt to wherever she ventured.

Paballo whispered into Mahali's ear so that the other waiting passengers would not hear. She said, 'Mahali, I have to go to the ladies' room. Just remain with the child and look after the bundles. Keep counting them.' The urge to visit the toilet had suddenly made her aware of the many people around and the pungent smell which emanated from the rows of closed doors and the impatient faces of the women who were awaiting their turns.

When she returned, Mahali looked at her with a smile. She had already thought of a solution to their problem. Before Paballo had squeezed herself into 'her place' on the bench, Mahali stammered, 'I know what we shall do, Aunty. Before it becomes too late for us to find a place. . . . "A re e o kopa boroko ha Nkhono Mm'a-Letia".'

'How *can* we?' Paballo asked, raising her shoulders in despair.

Mahali could not understand. She always found Grandmother Mm'a-Letia smiling and happy to see them whenever they went visiting there. She wondered why her aunt was hesitant to go to her house and 'ask for sleep'.

With an earnest face, Paballo asked Mahali, 'Are you aware just how much Aunt Mm'a-Letia struggles in that house of hers, Mahali? Ever since her daughter Letia died, she has had to raise her two granddaughters and grandson besides caring for Thabo her own son. The two granddaughters are the only ones who sometimes help her with some money; but those two men – Thabo and Keletso – just do not bother. There are only four small rooms like ours, and there are already five adults sleeping there. How shall we all squeeze ourselves and our luggage in there?'

Mahali thought of Thabo and Keletso. She nodded, remembering the 'names' by which they were known to the youth in the township. Thabo, known as 'Bra Tabs', was in fact her 'uncle' in the extended family tree; and Keletso was popularly known as 'Keltz'. How ugly these names became when they were distorted! Mahali shook her head, remembering that according to custom, *she* would have to regard her Uncle Thabo as 'Malome-mo-ja-lihloho' (the one who is answerable to all her life's 'affairs', who has to carry out all the ritual require-ments as prescribed). How would these 'lost' couldn't-care-less, yet valuable and irreplaceable members of the extended family cope when *their* turn came?

Paballo realised that she had to 'educate' her niece, lest she be 'lost' like so many of her generation. 'Mahali, you must know all your relatives so that one day when you cannot find happiness and success in your matters, you know where to "run to". It is important for you to know that you are not alone, that you are never an "orphan". There is always someone in the "family" who is under obligation to "stand" by you. These are your people, your own flesh and blood. They cannot turn away from their duties no matter how irresponsible they may be. It is their blood that counts.'

'Yes, Aunty. But how are we to work together when we never even meet? Look, I had even forgotten that there are such people at Grandma Mm'a-Letia's. When-ever we go visiting there, they are never there. In fact

I've always thought that they live somewhere far away.
Even on Sundays we never find them. Are they aware
that sometime in the future when some of us have
"matters" to be dealt with, they'll have to live up to the
demands of custom? Do they know these rituals at all?'

'It is just that things are so much more difficult to
organise, Mahali. They *are* aware of these 'laws' because
the elders always "preach" about them. The word is not
the finger, it does not go and come back, it stays . . .
"Lentsoe ha se monoana, ha le e e le khutla", you know
that, don't you. Just like I am telling you all these
things, "tomorrow" *you'll* be telling your children,
those who come after you. If we throw away our rituals
we are as good as dead. No one can succeed in
destroying us if we know ourselves and those "laws"
that our ancestors have left us with.

'When their turn comes, people like your Uncle
Keletso will realise that *they* too will never find peace
and their "affairs" will never succeed because their
"duties" are not fulfilled. The spirits of the ancestors
will never set them free. They will be bound to abide
by the "rules". You must realise that they are being
tossed around by difficulties which they encounter. "Ba
thefuloa ke lifefo tsa bophelo." But of course that does
not mean that they have to give in to problems. It is
their duty to fight them. Aunt Mm'a-Letia is also not
without blame because she allows these young people
to trample over her. What she should do is to insist that
they respect her. She should not allow them to toss her
around. Perhaps it is because she is getting on in years
and they know that their other elders are far away and
unable to come and "speak to them". It is high time
someone from our uncles and big-Fathers straightened
them up. They are like carnivorous animals which move
at night. They hunt for places where they can find

something to drink. Then they stumble home to Mm'a-Letia's when the biting early winds force them to find a place where they can cuddle. When they wake up hungry, they open empty pots and beg, or even demand food from 'Mm'a-Letia. Big men expect their elderly grandmother and mother to feed them – it's wrong! How can we now go to add on to Aunt Mm'a-Letia's problems, Mahali? How can we ask for sleep at her place? Mind you, she would never turn us away because it is also her "duty" to welcome me when I "come crying" to her according to custom and blood, but really, I feel for her "mosali-moholo oa molimo". She is my mother's own sister.'

'Does Grandma Mm'a-Letia feed such big men from her lousy pension money?'

'Yes, she does. If it were not for the help she gets from her granddaughters Grace and Neo they would really starve. Grace is a nurse-aid at Baragwanath Hospital and Neo has a clerical job in town.

'If we go there, there'll be nowhere for us to sleep. Chairs and tables would have to be packed in some corner to make room for us. We would perhaps have to sleep in the kitchen. But even then, the little space in the kitchen is virtually a passage as you know. Everyone going out or coming in walks through the kitchen. It means they'll have to jump and hop over us. I shall never find sleep. And I have to wake up and go to work in the morning and leave you to look after Mzwandile. It means that you'll have to stay away from school. You'll have to go to school some time in the day and report to the Principal that you had to look after the child. We shall have to say that you had to take "Zwandie" to the clinic, what shall we do? I cannot stay away from work because we need the money.'

Paballo thought silently for a while and shook her

head vigorously. She muttered, 'No Mahali, we cannot go to Aunt Mm'a-Letia's place, we can't. She has her hands full. Her own son Thabo – your uncle – drinks heavily. What if he should trip over us and fall? Imagine what would happen if he fell on little Zwandie? And Keletso seems to have taken after Thabo too. He must be thinking it is "manly" to go about doing nothing but drinking all day and night. Those two never even help to do chores around the house. They are not even ashamed to see old Mm'a-Letia struggle to do the garden with her "arthritis" and everything.'

'No Aunty, I can see that we cannot go and "ask for sleep" there. What shall we do?'

Paballo thought seriously. She was just about to say something when she stopped abruptly, winced and twisted her face. Mahali noticed her aunt's distorted face and snapped uneasily, 'What's wrong, Aunty?'

Unmistakable. She sat poised, as if listening. It was the first signal, the early quickening of the new life within her. It was a disturbing sensation. Prior to the events of the past hours which had led to her leaving her home unexpectedly, not a minute had passed when she did not remember that she was pregnant once more. The devastating confirmation she had received from the clinic doctor had left her confused and uncertain whether to rejoice or to cry.

With the additional responsibility of caring for another baby she would have to stop working. Being at work at certain hours of the day granted her the very-much-needed break to be away from the stress and strain of being with her in-laws, the inevitable outcome of sharing her small house with them. Their unconcealed hostility towards her clouded her mind day and night. What shattered her even more was the fact that Musi, her husband, had not received the announcement that

17

they were expecting another child enthusiastically either. She remembered that she was now eighteen weeks pregnant and that the 'signals' she was now feeling would develop into violent kicks as time went by, never giving her time to forget that she should prepare for a new life.

Paballo felt even more alone. The ground over which she was resting seemed to have shifted away, leaving her hanging over a ghastly chasm. She should have known better, she thought bitterly. Deep in her heart she was reprimanding herself. . . . "Leoto ha le na nko; ha le nkhelle." The foot does not have a nose; it does not smell out. The foot carries you even to the thresholds of your enemies. It even takes you and deposits you at the very edge of a precipice and you can watch helplessly as you dangle and your hopes for survival are sinking into the depths of despair.

It was Mahali who broke the uneasy silence. She spoke softly so that the people around would not hear. She said, 'Honestly if one day I should marry, I'll insist that my in-laws live in their own house far away from my husband and I, honestly. If they force matters and come to where I am, I'll leave them and get another house.'

Her aunt was a little annoyed at what Mahali had said. She retorted, 'You really speak like a child, Mahali. You think it's easy for a woman like myself (or a man, for that matter) just to bolt out when it is tough and get yourself another place. What about the law? What about the whole set-up of locations and superintendents and black-jacks and the waiting lists and so on? Besides, under the law, I would have to get my husband's permission. What if he should refuse, even if there *was* "another place or house" as you say?'

'Of course he would refuse because he is not having

any problems putting up with his people. *I* would leave him immediately, honestly, Aunty.'

'What about your children: what would you say to them? You are able to talk like that because you are now old enough to understand what is happening. What about Zwandie here, for instance? Even now as we are sitting here he understands nothing. He has already asked so many times when we are going back home.'

'I am sorry, Aunty, if what I said offended you. I suppose I do not understand, just like Zwandie.'

Mahali excused herself and moved in the direction of the stench, where some women were waiting in an unending queue to go in the toilets. She stood there shaking her head. The whole thing of marriage and in-laws and houses and laws and superintendents was all too confusing and annoying at the same time. What does being a woman mean to everybody, to the laws anyway, she wondered, tears of remorse filling her eyes. With the back of her hand, she wiped the tears away and was thankful that she was a good distance away from her aunt.

Mahali sat next to her aunt and said nothing. Paballo gave her a bank-note which she had dug out of her purse. 'Just go and buy us two more cold drinks. You know what I like . . . lemonade.' Of late Paballo had been drinking virtually gallons of the stuff. 'Buy yourself one too if you like.'

Mahali smiled and shook her head. She remarked, 'I've been drinking too many Cokes, Aunty; I'd like something to eat – a hamburger. Don't you feel like eating something? You've never ate anything since this morning when we arrived here. We were all looking forward to having a good Saturday lunch meal with that soup as an "introduction". The soup was smelling so good. Those herbs and bayleaves we added into it really smelt good and inviting. I couldn't wait to taste it . . . and then it happened . . . everything was spoilt.'

As Mahali left for their refreshments, her aunt reminded her, 'Don't buy any more ice-creams for Zwandie, Mahali. He has already had too many of them. Get him something to eat too.'

She did not want to speak nor remember what had happened before she and her niece had left the house with the bundles on their heads. She felt a little uneasy and ashamed. What did anyone in their street who had seen them carrying bundles on their heads, like old Sophiatown washerwomen, think, she wondered. No matter how much she tried, her mind clung on to those moments like a nightmare. She had tried hard to dispel those thoughts about her quarrel with Musi. It was striking to her what little provocation it took of late to get them bickering at each other. He seemed so much more impatient, and ready to take her to task more than ever before. Is it true, she wondered, that 'monna o hlalisoa mosalie', that when a woman is expecting a baby, her husband feels a certain aversion towards her, and that he usually finds himself unable to do anything about it? But the quarrels and bickering started long long ago when Zwandie was only a baby. In fact she could even trace them to when they started living under the same roof with his people. The removals of his parents from the farm Klipgat in the northern Transvaal had forced them to come to their son in Soweto. Musi could not bear to stand by while his elderly parents were being shunted around from one bare veld to another.

Paballo recalled Musi's loud clanging offensive voice echoing through the kitchen that morning. It seemed to hit the rafters above, then knock against the iron roofing and bounce back to her with the momentum and thunder it gathered as it traversed through space. He bellowed at her, '. . . And can someone tell me just why that damned pot of soup keeps boiling away? For goodness' sake why can't someone dish out for my parents anyway?'

He had not even bothered to find out how she had struggled to get the food in the pots in the first place. She had had no time to think clearly. All she knew was that she had to go out of their lives once and for all! Is that why the old women sit and tell you to 'giny'ilitye', swallow the stone, when you get married? That you as a woman should overlook whatever unpleasant and painful things happen to you in marriage and bear it all out like a soldier, she wondered. 'Well I just could not go on taking it any more,' Paballo mumbled to herself. 'It just does not matter how much you sacrifice, they always regard you as a "ngoetsi", "makoti" – something with no feelings like a stone!'

Mahali had yet another brain-wave. She was excited and smiling when she made the suggestion. She snapped, 'What about Kwa-Thema, Aunty? We could go to Ntate-moholo Tsitso's place. The last time, we "ran" to his place, didn't we?'

'That's far away in Springs. And that was only possible because I was on leave at the time when we quarrelled with Musi and he drove me away. I've thought of it too; but then I have to come to work here in Johannesburg every morning. It's not possible Mahali . . . very expensive too. Uncle Tsitso is in fact "Malome-mo-ja-lihloho", my eldest maternal uncle who has to make decisions on matters concerning my welfare.'

'Ntate-moholo Tsitso is not aware that you are still having all these problems; that we still run around having to "look for sleep" with "lithoto" balanced on our heads. Or have you ever written to him to tell him that things still have not changed?'

Mahali shook her head. She added sadly, 'What hurts most is that at the time, it was decided by Musi's people that they would pay the "fine" of an ox imposed on them by my people for "ill-treatment" and for Musi's audacity in driving me out of my own house. That fine was never paid, and now we're back to square one.'

'Ao! It was never paid? I was too young to understand but I never asked because as youngsters one is not allowed to probe and question affairs of elderly people. Now what is the use if in-laws do not respect the rulings of the people? It means that anything can happen to you as "ngoetsi". What shall we do now, Aunty?'

Paballo reflected for a while and replied, 'I was just thinking that because it is already becoming late and the traffic of commuters is increasing, and because we have these bundles to carry, we must go back to Soweto.'

'Back to Dube and those people, Aunty, back to your house?'

'No, Mahali. Let's go to my brother – your Uncle Mpempe in Molapo township. He will help me sort everything out. I did not want to upset him because he gets quite irritated seeing me "looking for sleep" all over the place because of what happens between me and Musi. But now I have nowhere to go to at the moment. I have to find some place. We must find a place to sleep. Zwandie is tired and sleepy.'

It was a relief to Mahali that her Aunty had finally made a decision. She immediately picked up Zwandie from Paballo's lap and strapped him on her own back. She suggested, 'OK, Aunty, I'll take Zwandie and two bundles and you can take the rest.'

Paballo was thankful for Mahali's nearness and for

her very understanding and considerate nature. Deep in her heart, she prayed that her niece should not meet with the kind of problems she was now experiencing. As she bent down to pick up her two bundles, she could already feel inside her the discomfort caused by the additional 'bundle', and the tightening of the muscles in her groin. She sighed and whispered, 'Let's go.'

By the time Mahali and Paballo got off the bus at the 'Pietersburg' stop on the outskirts of Rockville township, it was dark. With the help of a few sympathetic passengers, they managed to roll the bundles through the narrow passage, out of the bus and on to the gravel pavement.

The smell of smoke from the chimneys and the grey dust raked up as the vehicles sped along Vundla Drive hit their nasal passages. They did not notice the silvery moon above, across whose face clouds of smog were drifting and playing hide and seek. They trudged along anxiously.

It was important that they keep moving because it was becoming late. Paballo heaved the one big bundle and deposited it on the crown of her head so that her neck jerked backwards. She steadied herself by keeping her legs astride. For the first time since she and Mahali had taken to the street, tears of bitterness flooded her eyes and she wished that her parents were still alive. Had she truly been reduced to a mere lingerer carrying bundles of clothing balanced on her head, she wondered. Never in her whole life did she even dream that such a thing would happen to her.

From the noise coming through the open windows of Mpempe's house, it was evident that they had many visitors. It would not be good behaviour for the tear-stained face of a woman to appear suddenly before a rowdy, jovial 'crowd'. The two women hesitated. Paballo, in her feminine wisdom, stepped aside at the gate and beckoned Mahali to follow her. In the shadowy protection of the hedge fence, they relieved themselves of the bundles and wiped their sweaty brows. Roars of laughter mingled with yells of female voices punctuated an incoherent chorus of music and ululating. Paballo felt uneasy that her own sadness would immediately transform the exaltation of her brother's 'family' into dejection. This was not to happen; she would make sure of that. She whispered to her niece, 'Mahali, you go in and call Mpempe. Be careful not to attract the attention of the visitors. Make sure that no one overhears you. Tell him that I'm here. Tell my brother that I would like to speak to him.'

An hour later, Mpempe knocked impatiently on the front door of Paballo's house. His sister and Mahali looked at each other, an atmosphere of uncertainty preying on their minds. They stood quietly and waited with the bundles still balanced on their heads. All Mpempe wanted was to resolve the whole matter of what he called 'the repeated degradation of his sister'. This time he had come to confront his brother-in-law man to man!

It was Musi's father who opened the door. The three went into the house and stood at the door. Mpempe, suppressing his anger, informed the old man that he had come to see Musi. He impatiently explained the purpose of his 'visit'. All the old man could say was, 'Musi left early in the afternoon. He said that he was going to look for his wife.'

His eyes rested on Paballo's face for a while. The three put the bundles on the floor almost simultaneously.

Mpempe sighed uneasily as he went through the whole process of explanation. All he wanted was to settle the matter with his brother-in-law *once and for all*, he emphasised. The old man, on the other hand, implored him to have the whole matter deferred to a later time 'when the elderly people on both sides can resolve the matter'.

There was no point in trying to speak to these old people, Mpempe felt, shaking his head. They will hold on to the stumps of a tree even when leaves are long squashed dead and the branches are only dry twigs.

'Tell your son that he has had a very narrow escape,' Mpempe murmured into the face of the bewildered old man.

Somehow Paballo knew that the planned meetings would never take place. All her uncles were now too ill or too old to deal effectively with Musi's people. She knew that she was back to square one. Her brother had assured her that he would settle the matter man to man. That she saw as her only hope. It was becoming more and more difficult to work things 'our way' – the respectable traditional way.

Mahali sat down and transferred Mzwandile on to her lap. He was fast asleep and untouched by all that was happening. For him it had been a long, long day of drifting from pillar to post.

Mpempe shook his head and left. He would certainly be coming again, he said. Paballo looked around at the furniture and wondered whether she would ever find happiness within the walls of that dreary match-box. The bundles looked like objects which did not belong to the surroundings. She wondered why she had agreed to come back at all. But where would she have escaped to, she asked herself.

The old man looked at Mahali and the child and

smiled uneasily. He said, 'Mahali, put Mzwandile to sleep and take the bundles back into the bedroom. Let us all go to sleep.'

Inside the old people's bedroom, Paballo's mother-in-law sat with bated breath, waiting for her husband to come and inform her of what had happened. You never know what young people can do when they are angry, she said to herself. The old man entered and shut the door behind him. He smiled broadly and whispered into his wife's partially deaf ear, 'Thank God they are back. Where would we get all that money to pay another fine? Another ox!'

Exactly four-and-a-half months later, Paballo gave birth to a bunny baby girl. Musi's people named her Mm'a-lithoto, mother of bundles . . . yet another of Paballo's bundles of joy.

'Fud-u-u-a!' *

Dikeledi (or Nkele) hurried towards Park Station, Johannesburg. She mingled with the other pedestrians dodging, winding and scuttling along without slowing down. It was five-fifteen in the evening. She knew that she would arrive in time for the 'Six-Nine' – the First-Stop-Naledi train. The thought that Ntombi, her friend, would be anxiously waiting for her at the station made her smile.

It was never easy to make one's way through the hundreds of people, all competing for passing space. The two parallel streams on either side of Von Brandis Street looked like human avalanches. Nkele had avoided Eloff Street, thinking that Von Brandis would be better.

'Ke semphete-ke-go-fete ka Morena!' Nkele remarked. We are like bees, she complained softly to herself, pausing for a split second before she crossed

---

* A chant sung by distressed commuters trying to get on to crowded trains. They turn their backs to the train entrances and wriggle their bottoms in order to make a space for themselves as they chant 'F-u-d-u-u-a!'

Pritchard Street, and holding tightly on to the straps of her shopping bag.

It was mainly black faces. She dismissed with a smile the thought which came flashing into her mind that most whites seemed of late to avoid moving along the main thoroughfares leading towards Park Station at that time of day. She mused at the thought of the many arguments which often resulted in black-versus-white free-for-alls at such times. She remembered, chuckling, how she herself would become involved in the skir-mishes, all through the shuffling and colliding of opposing waves of human traffic – whites maintaining that the blacks should remember to stick to their 'place' by keeping 'out of the way' and the blacks stubbornly refusing to accept the 'order' and dismissing it as a sign of nonsensical arrogance! The adjacent never-ending 'flood' of cars in the street itself only aggravated matters. What would happen if the traffic lights were not there, Nkele asked herself reflecting, and allowing her mind to wander freely. It was a typical Friday evening.

'Shall I make it?' she asked herself, wondering doubt-fully. She was going to take a chance and leap into Jeppe Street just as the robot was about to turn red against her when someone reached for her elbow, and held her back softly. She had kept moving and moving without presence of mind. If it had not been for the timely gesture of the man, Nkele would have darted right into the flow of cars which came in rushing impetuously down that street. She stopped abruptly and gasped thankfully, 'Dankie Abuti!' She sighed, looking up at the face of the person whose arm had steadied her and had perhaps saved her from certain disaster. 'Our brothers are usually *so* protective towards us in town here,' Nkele thought, gratefully. When the green light came on, she hurried on, shuffling, brushing and bumping against one person after another.

Again the question kept creeping into her mind . . . 'Shall I make it?' she asked herself once more. 'That stupid Boer guard of the "Six-Nine" has the filthy habit of blowing the whistle a whole three, even four minutes before "ten to"; A ka go seleka!' (He can make you fed-up) Nkele remarked, adding, 'Kajeno ho na ha ke *batle* ho e supa ka monoana, ka Morena!' (Today of all days I do not *want* to point at it with my finger, honestly.) 'Not on a *Friday* – and it's even *month-end* for that matter.' Nkele whispered to herself, 'Thank God I did all my shopping during lunch-time. At least this week I will not have to come to town tomorrow for shopping.'

It had been one of those rare 'good' Fridays when the white woman (their wage clerk) had been in a happy mood to hand the black staff their pay envelopes before lunch-time.

The pressure exerted by the straps on her fingers became increasingly unbearable and she transferred the heavy bag from one arm to the other. She repeated the act of alternating almost automatically.

The familiar Friday-evening 'stampede' for trains, buses or taxis, etc. had now become, to her, like the other commuters, just one of those phenomena one had to live with and fight one's way through. One had to be alert all the time. She quickly stepped into the station concourse in the direction of the line of the temporary stalls the black women had erected to display fruits and other wares. They were smiling and chatting with each other. They, too, were alert, all the time keeping an eye on their merchandise – apples, pears, oranges, naartjies, peanuts, which were neatly arranged in attractive cone-shaped little hillocks. 'Business is good,' Nkele imagined they might be saying to each other, peering at each other through the throngs of passing commuters, some of whom stopped now and then to buy.

The fruit-sellers were obviously in a good mood, and they had reason to be thankful too. The white policemen in their usual packed pick-up vans, who always seemed to appear from God-knows-where, had not come today. The women were smiling, watching and giving each other all the moral support women in need of help *ought* to give each other. 'We're all alike; we're women. We need each other when things are difficult because we have given birth to children. Wherever one goes one hears women say, 'we have to feed our children, haven't we?' On this particular day, a Friday which also fell on the last day of the month, the 'white dogs' (as they refer to the white police) had not dashed in to kick the rows of boxes on which the women had exhibited their hard-earned wares. They had not come to load the hawkers mercilessly on to the pick-up vans and disappear swearing and threatening. At times they would just smash and destroy the products, throwing them into the nearest rubbish cans and trampling maliciously over them in disgust. The persistence and determination of the women was a pain in the necks of the police especially because whenever they chased them, they never succeeded in getting hold of them. They would vanish without a trace into the black myriads in the corridors and station platforms. And one black face looks exactly like another when one is confronted with the task of identifying them from the milling thousands. What is worse, in the spirit of black solidarity, the passengers *never* helped to expose the 'offenders'!

Nkele smiled. Ntombi must be waiting, she pondered. There is nothing like the knowledge that the help of another woman is available to you whenever you need it, when the going gets tough, as the saying goes. Ntombi was her bosom friend. It had been like that for years, ever since she left school and started travelling to work in town on board the Soweto trains. And now they were both married and they had children to work for.

All Nkele needed to be conscious of was that she had her shopping bag; that everything was meticulously packed with every packet squeezed in so that nothing would be damaged along the journey. She remembered that she had checked the zip again and again to make sure that it *did* work. And her *purse* . . . of course her purse with all that had remained after she had bought what she thought were essentials for the weekend was *inside*. It was *right inside . . . on her person*, over her *pubis – in between her pantihose and her tight step-in corset!* No one could get his hand in there. The purse was quite safe there. Anyone who would have the guts to dig in there would be very brave indeed. She would scream and by the time he got hold of the purse, she would have made so much noise that people all around would come to her aid. No pick-pocket would want to be the centre of attraction. She and Ntombi would help each other. They would stand face to face in the train, clasping their shopping bags tightly against their legs and breathing over each other's shoulder *and watching*. 'You need to have someone to see what is happening behind you too,' Nkele mumbled to herself, her face brightening into a broad smile.

Just as she descended the second flight of stairs on Platforms 1 and 2, the whistle went, its shrill piercing sound stabbing painfully right through her heart. She nearly stood dead still. In fact she might have done so if it had not been for the force of the moving 'stream' behind her. The 'torrent' of male passengers tore even more hastily past her, forcing her – amid loud squeals of female voices – to 'float' towards the wall. If all this was taking place on a race track, one would have imagined the whistle to have given the final take-off 'Go' signal!

'Die bleddie naalertjie van 'n vark; ons sal hom wys!' (Bloody swine; we'll teach him a lesson.) Some cursed loudly as they sprinted past, others hurling their sprightly figures over the sloping walls, landing over the edge of the platform, and expertly making it into the moving train. Others jumped over two, and sometimes three steps at a time to scale the distance. To them it was just one of those things. They swore, 'Die hond; hy wil ons los!' but they knew all the time that they would get into the train, come what may. And as they gasped, adjusting their jackets, they pointed accusing fingers towards the rear of the moving train where the uncaring pink face of the guard was just disappearing.

Nkele's delicate body had been pressed against the hard wall for what seemed like hours when in fact it could only have been for half a minute. She had kept her eyes shut, holding on to her bag with all her might. Someone had clung on to her. From the faint subdued squeaking cries the person had made, she knew that it was a woman. The distressed stranger had dug her face into the nape of Nkele's neck. When the weight on her back started easing off slowly, poor Nkele was relieved because she knew that the worst was over.

'I'm sorry, my sister. I hope I didn't break all your bones,' the woman apologised, their eyes meeting and smiling into each other. She was a little older than Nkele, and she tugged at her sleeve, indicating the desire to help her carry the heavy bag. Together they scuttled quickly out of the way, moving as carefully as they could and as closely to the wall as possible. At the end of the stairs, the two hustled away from the joggling, propelling throngs and sought momentary shelter in the angle formed by the tall concrete pillar and the wall.

'Come, my sister, let us whisper,' the kind strange woman proposed, just as Ntombi was making her way towards them. Ntombi was twisting and pushing, struggling to disentangle herself from the nest of 'wrestling' bodies. She shouted, 'Nkele o e, Nkele!' to her friend.

'Oh, there's Ntombi. She's my friend. She'll help me. Thanks and don't worry; I'll . . .'

The other interrupted her, 'It's all right, Nkele my sister. Let Ntombi come along. Both of you. Come Ntombi; my name is Mashadi. Come, let us whisper. This corner here looks safer. They won't crush us here.' The three laughed loudly. There were no formal introductions necessary. Women in distress just accept each other without much hesitation because they know that they *need* each other.

'Re basadi bo batlhe; tlaeang re itshebeng' (we are all women; come, let us whisper to one another), Shadi repeated, retreating deeper into the 'safe' nook. 'What shall we do? The "Six-Nine" has left us; so we have to wait for the "O-Five".'

Nkele was disappointed. She very much regretted the 'unfortunate' occurrence. She remarked, 'We really have *no* luck today. . . . That silly guard, fancy just letting the "Six-Nine" take off like that. And a whole three minutes before time. Now we have no alternative but to take the "O-Five" – and I *hate* going into that train!' She turned to her friend. 'Shame. You must have been looking around for me, Ntombi my dear.'

The other nodded in response, adding, 'Yes, Nkele my sister. But don't worry. We shall make it somehow. You know we are used to fighting. And you, Shadi my sister, you were going to tell us something weren't you?

You had something on your mind, let's hear it. We're women. We're all alike.'

Shadi looked around, stammering reluctantly, 'You know . . . I *hate* the "O-Five", I never want to set my foot in it! Come, listen; we have to whisper. I don't want the other people to hear us. I once had a most nasty experience on the "O-Five".'

Ntombi could not stand the suspense any longer, and she wondered what it was all about. She asked, 'What nasty experience? Tell us. You'll be surprised to find that we know all about it. That we have also had even worse experiences, my sister, tell us. There's too much noise. People are straining their ears trying to hear what the announcer is saying. Sometimes I wonder why they introduce that howler at all!'

The three women looked around them. The usual Friday evening 'stampede' was at its peak. The formal announcements seemed quite useless on such days. They only served to confuse passengers all the more. In any case, most of the people were either too excited or too involved in their own varied conversations to listen. Even what was said over the loudspeaker was not always reliable. *'Anything can happen!'* you would hear a person say, annoyed. 'You come rushing into Platforms 1 and 2, and you see the train you want unashamedly rattle right over on to the other side into Platform *"voetsek"* and you have to jump over rails and break your legs or lose your life, just like that. They don't care! You just have to be on the alert and read the train numbers yourself!'

No one was listening to the announcer. He bellowed the numbers and the words away, melodiously adding twists of tone, 'crooning' in a heavy bass like he was imitating Paul Robeson and failing hopelessly. It *could* be that he, too, had the 'Friday fever'. He was sitting there with his pay packet in front of him, serenading to it, and enjoying listening to his own voice.

Nkele reminded Mashadi, urging impatiently, 'You were still telling us by the way, Mashadi my sister. We shall just have to go into the "O-Five". There is nothing we can do. . . . OK, what happened? Go on.'

Shadi tried hesistantly to proceed. The words just would not come out. She gurgled, 'It happened on the train . . . the "O-Five". I was not aware what had happened. I did not feel anything at the time, you see. The train was packed and everyone was sandwiched into everyone as usual. The train kept swaying from side to side as if the wheels had moved out of place . . . "gadl-ang-gadlang, gadlang-gadlang, gadlang-gadlang", it was noisy, you know . . .'

The others nodded, smiling sympathetically. Shadi was amazed. She asked, 'He bathong, le a tshega?' (People are you laughing?)

'Siza'thini Shadi my sister? It hurts so much. . . . What's the use of crying?' Ntombi asked.

This very sad sensitive subject, sparked off by Mashadi's dilemma, was not merely an isolated case. It was a painful harrowing experience, always related in bated breath by helpless misused and derogated bitter women of all ages.

There was complete silence. Each one of the women was thinking what they would now have to do. They would have to keep together and give each other moral (and as far as possible) physical support as well. One had to be strong to face the daily hazards of travelling in the trains of Soweto.

Ntombi was sad and bitter. She wondered why they, the black women who were trying to make a living, should be victims of all the evil in the land. She spoke softly and said, 'We all know about these terrible occurrences, Shadi my dear, and are only smiling because "baholo ba re loso leholo ke ditshego" – people laugh even when they are under the threat of death. It happens all the time and we have no way of fighting against it.'

Ntombi declared, 'What is annoying about this congestion is that you never see it happening in *their* trains – those "whites only" coaches. They make sure that the white passengers sit comfortably. You very rarely find them standing even at the very busy hours like early in the morning when most people board trains, and at this time of night when everybody wants to go home. Sometimes this very difference between "black" and "white" is so bad that it can easily lead to a "black" against "white" war. Look at what happens in the trains serving Randfontein, Krugersdorp, Roodepoort, Pretoria and so on. See what the "white" coaches are like as compared to the "black" ones. The carriages for whites are always *so* many! Why can't they have more for blacks when we are so many, why? They provide more for people who do not need them; like with the buses in town. This whole one-sided way of treating people can sometimes be dangerous. You know one day in the morning when "our" sardine-like packed train got to the Langlaagte junction, the "comfortable all-white Randfontein train" was just crossing on to the other line and the two moved side-by-side. Some of the whites on *their* train were looking at us smiling as if they were sneering at monkeys in the zoo. As if we were deliberately put there for their entertainment.'

Before Ntombi could continue with her story, Nkele and Shadi were already smiling in that 'we-know-it-all' manner. Nkele, unable to restrain herself from interrupting her, added, 'Yes, of course they would . . . the same way they bring white tourists into Soweto in luxury buses to come and "study" us like their mute animals.'

'On that day, we nearly saw something terrible. The young men in our train became irritated and abusive. They hurled insult after insult at them: "Komaan, maak jou groen oë toe, jou lelike nyoertjie!" . . . "Jy lag jou bleddie fokken Boer!" . . . (Cummon – face your front, you swine!) . . . It went on like that. People lose their self-respect when they are made to feel like they are dogs. There was nothing anyone could do to calm them down. They were *furious!* They even wanted to throw knives and other dangerous weapons at them (you know they carry such things on the trains, especially on week-ends). The whites were wise enough to draw the blinds to prevent serious fighting from starting. . . . You know what I mean. Anything could happen.'

Just then Mashadi interjected, 'Honestly they treat us *just like dogs.*'

'*Even dogs are better, my sister,*' Nkele emphasised sadly. 'They don't treat dogs like that; they *nurse* them like small babies. They even give us rotten "dogs' meat" – what they would rather not give to their dogs.'

'Yes, I know,' Ntombi agreed, adding, 'In their "kitchens". It's awful, I know.'

The three watched the Pimville-Midday-Line trains come and go, and the jostling and rubbing and the deafening noise continued. They were looking on and reflecting, anxiously awaiting *their* turn to be caught up in what was virtually the 'front line' of a black woman's battle for mere existence in the bustling city of gold. Ntombi broke the uneasy silence again, her voice penetrating the variable sounds all around them. Her mind had suddenly gone back, focussing on experiences she and her bosom friend had had; the very first battle they had fought and which had cemented them into practically a team of comrades in action. She recalled, 'The limit was the early morning "Four-Six" First-Stop-Braamfontein. Do you remember, Nkele?' she asked, looking at her friend and smiling.

'What happened, people, *tell me*,' Mashadi pleaded, looking from the one to the other of her companions.

'How can I ever forget that?' Nkele enquired parenthetically. She narrated, 'It was just after I had left school and got my first job. I *had* to take the Naledi "Four-Six". *Moo* ke ntoa e a lefu le bophelo, ke u joetsa, my sister' (*there*, it is a battle for life and death, let me tell you). 'I remember seeing "*the thing*" for the first time. I saw "the veterans"(bo-Nkatha ba basadi) – women who had become tough and brave – remove their wigs and stockings and stuffing them into their handbags as we approached Naledi Station. . . . You remember those days black women used to wear wigs?'

The others nodded, smiling expectantly. Nkele proceeded. 'When the train came bouncing into that Naledi platform, I was surprised to see people turn their backs away from the doors ready to propel with their shoulder-blades and backsides. "Fudua! . . . fudua! . . . fudu-a-a!" (stir the pot! st-i-i-r the p-o-t!), the push-push yelling started as everyone, man, woman and child alike, strained all the muscles in their bodies to get inside. I just allowed myself to be "carried" along. I thought I would be flattened dead by the time I got inside. On that "Four-Six", no one dares sit down on the hard wooden benches. Everyone in the coaches has to stand, on the benches or on the floor. You did what everybody else was doing if you did not want to break your back or lose your limbs. . . . I jumped on to the bunk and was forced into that upright position by the many bodies around me. All along, when I was being "carried", I could feel that my clothes were moving from around my calves upwards and there was nothing I could do to lower them. How *could* I? . . . I *had* to keep my arms firmly crossed over my breasts all the time because I had to make sure my handbag would not "drift" away from me. It was *then* that I saw Ntombi. The poor girl's face was flushed as if someone had dipped it in boiling water. Her hair, which had been neatly brushed, was now "standing" in unkempt irregular heaps. Although it was winter, there was steam all over inside the train, caused by the vapours from the mouths and nostrils of the passengers and the closed windows. The windows were closed because otherwise the ice-cold air would rush in and those standing near them would suffer. So we remained in that upright position, and the train took off.

'Someone – a woman – started singing a hymn. Her voice was sharp and loud. I tried to turn my head to see her but so many people were packed and squeezed against each other that it was impossible to see her. Soon after, other voices, women's voices, joined in the singing. They were singing a hymn from the popular apostolic hymnals – "Lifela tsa Sione".

' "Hosanna ho Morena!" (Praise be to the Lord!) Yet another woman yelled loudly, like someone already possessed by the holy spirit.

' "Amen, Alleluya!" The men and more women shouted loudly in reply.

' "Khotso ha e be ho batho!" (Peace be unto the people!) she cried in a piercing voice as if in thankful appreciation to the welcome response from the men. The people answered, joining eagerly in the singing.

' "Peace! Alleluya! Amen!" everybody roared.

'There was a whole deafening chorus. But at that moment, I really wished they would stop singing and praying. . . .'

Women, irrespective of whether they have children of their own or not, are always 'mothers'. At a critical moment, when they find themselves plunged into an awkward precarious situation, they become immediately inventive and they rally around one another. *Then* they cease to be 'childlike' but they appeal to their 'latent' inner strength of character. . . . In this diabolical setting, there is a lot at stake. The moral strength of a whole proud nation is faced with a cruel challenge. The young, the weak, have to be guided along the correct path of *human* and not *animal* behaviour. . . . An urgent appeal to their *conscience* has to be made. . . .

Why do you think our regular church-goers are predominantly women? Why do you think in the 'whites only' 'kitchens' there is what is known as 'Sheila's Day' and we never hear of 'John's Day'? . . . I have never heard of '*white* "Sheila's Day" ' either. Why do you think on Thursday afternoons *our* black mothers leave every other activity, garb themselves in *holy consecrated garments* (Seaparo), and converge on *the altar* with the sole *united* purpose of praying ('Bo-'Mé-ba-Merapelo')? . . . Do you think the sins of the members of our black mothers' households as against those of the white mothers are much greater? . . . Never! . . . In fact the very opposite prevails!

It is precisely because "M'a-Ngoana o tšoara thipa ka bohaleng" (the child's *mother* grabs the sharp end of the knife). It is because *they* (our black mothers) have to 'carry the cross' on their seemingly frail shoulders. When the 'father' plods his way to the place of worship – more often than not – reasons other than those of the one who must 'grab the sharp end of the knife' impel him. It is the black mothers who must pay the ultimate penalty. . . . No black mother (or even a snow-white one for that matter) will stand by and bear to watch passively while her young go to ruin without facing the foe herself.

We forgive our black mothers in their sad predicament for resorting to the ecumenical spear. It is perhaps the only 'weapon' they are familiar with. It is certainly the only one they are ever so readily offered to arm themselves with whenever they have to carry out an onslaught. . . .

'Those who could lift up their hands, started clapping them – *hard*. I wanted the music to stop because, instead of helping, the very noise was being used as a "shield". I was trying to scream that someone was busy massaging my thighs and backside, trying to probe into my private parts and nobody was paying attention. It was embarrassing and awful! That day, I thanked God for having given me big powerful thighs because all I did was cross them over one another and squeeze as hard as I could. I clenched my teeth and wished that I were *grinding* those fingers between my thighs. You see, with so much congestion, it was impossible to see who the culprits were. We suffocated and suffered in that terrible torture of it all, and there was nothing we could do. By the time the train got to Park Station, we were too hurt, too shamefully abused, to speak. Who could we speak to? Who could we accuse? Who would listen to us even if we tried to complain? Everyone would tell us that "it is all too shameful to say anything about this". I used to hear women *whisper* about this and never believed it. I used to hear them swearing and spitting. . . . On that day I remember hearing a number of powerless women cursing and shouting on the platform, adjusting the wigs on their heads and, like myself, trying their best to look lady-like and presentable. I resolved never to get on that "Four-Six" again. *That* day it was *our* turn, Ntombi, wasn't it?' Nkele asked, smiling and turning to her friend.

'Yes it *was*, and I'll never forget it as long as I live,' Nkele replied, smiling back thoughtfully. She remarked frowning, 'What is even more annoying is that no one wants to even *talk* about this whole "nonsense", as they regard it. It is *not* nonsense because who suffers? *We* suffer. They just don't care. They treat us exactly like animals.'

'Here's the "O-Five"!' someone shouted loudly. Others whistled. Nkele, Ntombi and Shadi scrambled into position. It was now time for business. Serious 'muscle' business; the tooth and nail fight for survival. 'Fudua! fudua! fud-u-u-u-a!' several gave the word of command.

Some youthful men wasted no time. Even before the train stopped, they held tightly on to the sides of the open windows, and swung their bodies, legs first, into the coaches. As soon as they had secured sitting space, they 'reserved' places for their female companions who of course had no alternative but to join the 'fudua' routine at the doorways. In another two to three minutes, the train had come to a complete standstill and the three women had succeeded somehow in battling their way in. They had at last found space to stand next to each other. It was an achievement and a victory which deserved to be celebrated. Alert and as watchful as ever, they stood smiling into each other's faces. They sighed. They had 'won'. . . . The whistle went. The "O-Five" rambled on and on noisily and 'indifferently' towards Naledi.

Dimomona

It was in Sophiatown on the early Monday morning of May 1932.

Boitumelo Kgope lay awake on the bed. It was a warm and comfortable bed. It was made up of a coir mattress over which a soft blanket was spread. He lay there with his eyes staring into the darkness. Although the room was pitch dark, he knew that it would soon be clearing.

He turned carefully so as not to awaken Dimomona, his lovely wife, lying fast asleep next to him. With his hand, he reached out and groped for the condensed-milk tin which served as a candle-stick. His fingers searched for the box of matches next to the tin and found it. Relying solely on his sense of touch, he stealthily scraped the rough surface of the match-box with the round head of the match-stick. He watched the tiny flame grow, its glow penetrating the darkness like someone suddenly opening a curtain. Dimomona's face was smiling peacefully and as beautiful as ever. He looked around at the room and its simple but neatly kept furniture. Everything was everywhere it always was. . . . Dimomona had hung his steam-pressed trousers over the bench ready for work. A box of cigarettes and his pass-book were next to the trousers. The room was arranged in 'sections'. These, under 'normal' circumstances, would have been four separate rooms of a semi-detached house – the kitchen, the bedroom, the dining-room portions. The different segments were easily identifiable because of the meticulous and orderly arrangement of the scanty furniture.

The Kgopes were tenants occupying one of a chain of ten rooms, each housing an average family of eight people. The couple were the only two people occupying their room because their three children and other members of their extended family were in Loskop, a so-called native reserve just 150 miles outside Greater Johannesburg. In fact, Dimomona had come to visit her husband for the sole purpose of conceiving their fourth child. 'Dimomona o ne a tlile goima' (she had come to 'fetch' another child). If it had not been for that 'sacred' reason, Boitumelo would have been alone busy working in Johannesburg.

The old 'Westclox' alarm-clock ticked away the seconds on the small table in the dining-room. It was ten to three. Boitumelo stared at his bicycle, the only article in the 'sitting-room' section besides his pair of white canvas shoes. Boitumelo was proud of the bicycle which made him the envy of most of the young men around that part of Sophiatown. The bicycle was indeed an object of beauty and wonder. He had himself spent the whole of the previous afternoon and evening cleaning it. He admired the shimmering framework, the steel tubing, the handlebars, the spokes of the wheels radiating from the central hub, shining like sunbeams. He had also polished the black rubber handles, the saddle-like seat and the black rubber foot pedals. The white pair of canvas shoes were scrubbed and dried in the sun. They sparkled like gems in the candle-light next to the bicycle where Dimomona had put them. They would contrast well with the black rubber pedals, he thought, smiling.

The bicycle was the most valuable item in the room, and because it was so treasured, it had to be guarded day and night. It was valued because it was 'precious'. And this was because it belonged, not to Boitumelo, but to his white boss. And his boss was the wealthy proprietor of a chain of dairies – the Golden City Dairies. Boitumelo was chief so-called delivery-boy at that prominent business establishment which supplied milk and related products to white homes, offices and firms in the whole of Johannesburg and its suburbs. He therefore had cause to be proud, especially of the bicycle which the boss allowed him to take with him after work.

When the first cocks started to take turns to crow, Boitumelo diligently stepped out of his floor-bed and quickly put on his pair of trousers. He knew that he would have to be the first one to open the doors of the firm so that the early milk deliveries could be made. As the so-called boss-boy he had to set an example to his subordinates. *That*, according to Boitumelo, was the way a man, a real man, should be judged. He went to the window, parted the flimsy calico curtain, and looked into the quiet partially lit yard. The row of rooms cast a long dark shadow into the yard. The street lamps only threw a semblance of light into the yard so that one could see the two bucket latrines situated next to the well. The silhouette of the pit-frame and the cement base were also visible. He would go and draw a pailful of water for Dimomona before he left for work. She was in an advanced state of pregnancy and he saw no reason why he should not help her although he was a man.

At the well, Boitumelo paused and looked around.
Not everyone was asleep at this early hour. It did not
surprise him to see windows with candle-light dotted in
several rooms even across Victoria Road. The smoke
from some braziers and chimneys was already swirling
round in woolly columns, pointing towards the starry
sky. He laid the pail on the cement platform and lit a
cigarette. He drew in long puffs and filled his lungs with
the cigarette smoke. He walked over to the nearest closet
and pushed the door cautiously. You never knew
whether there was someone in there or not. Some people
with nowhere to sleep were known to spend their nights
in the latrines. The door yielded easily and he went in.
It was always better to smoke while resting on the
wooden seat. That way, one did not inhale a lot of the
offensive fumes from the bucket underneath you. And
on Mondays the barrels were full to capacity.

There were subdued sounds and Boitumelo cocked
his ears to listen. All of a sudden, dogs started barking
and howling. One could hear them running in all directions. There was also a loud commotion of footsteps
and voices yelling insults – the all-too-familiar Boer
accent – all these could only mean one thing: it was yet
another of those police raids. And the unforgiveable
tragedy of it all was that Boitumelo had left his pass-
book on the bench in the room! A loud bang of a steel
bar against the toilet door meant that Boitumelo had to
finish whatever he was doing and walk out with his
arms held high above his head. He fumbled with his
trousers and the voice outside was impatient. It
screamed, 'Komaan, komaan jong – maak gou! Kom uit
nou!'

When he opened the door, the blinding torch-light
pointed into his eyes for a moment and he stumbled out
with his eyes shut. The whole yard was full of policemen

armed with steel bars, sjamboks and guns. It took time
for Boitumelo's eyes to adjust to the glare before him.
He could not believe that the whole place could, in a
shake of a duck's tail, be transformed into some kind
of siege. It was like a nightmare and he wished it would
soon end. But it did not. The voice went on, 'Komaan
pas jong . . . pas!'

In the street, mounted police, their guns pointing
into the air, moved restlessly about with heaving chests
across which the bandoliers were proudly strung. The
sparkling ends of the cartridges stuck out ominously
from the belts.

Dimomona walked alongside. She kept abreast with the
column from street to street. She had watched Boitumelo take his place in the cursed queue, the steel
manacles clasping his wrist tightly to another 'offender'.
She had witnessed it all from the other side of the street.
The 'induna' was waving a sjambok and cursing at the
top of his voice just like his masters. He repeated the
abuse in the faces of the 'newcomers' one by one:
'Komaan, uyangibheka? Ngena! Msatha-ka-nyoko!'
(Son of a bitch. 'Get into line and stop looking around!')

Boitumelo gave Dimomona a last glance and fell into
line, picking up the step. The die was cast. . . . Left,
right. . . . Left, right. . . . Left, right. . . . To the threshold of the house of damnation. From there it would
be 'Number Four', 'Blue Sky', or the Bethal farms. . . .

But first it was the rounds through dear Sophiatown.
The offenders had to be paraded so that others may see.
The others had to be frightened into obedience. Left,
right. . . . Left, right. . . . Left, right. . . . Forward
march!

At every corner, the 'induna' stopped the 'line' of
condemned men. They resembled a procession of yoked

oxen as they trudged along. Here and there, a captive held a tin containing a sample of the brew they were caught drinking – an exhibit to be put before the magistrate in court.

A sympathetic onlooker took heart and brought a shawl which she put over Dimomona's shoulders. It is not healthy or proper for a woman carrying so heavily to be cold and bare. The cold can be cunning, she reasoned; it can creep slowly down the spine into the burdened loins. It can crawl into the 'sacred bag' and affect the valued life, so that the young mother may experience difficulty in delivering safely. It is a matter for concern by all women, all mothers. Today it can be one woman's turn, and tomorrow it can be yours, or even your daughter's. What has befallen the Kgopes, their tragedy, is a tragedy for all. 'Bagolo ba re: matlo hosha mabapi' (the elders say: it is the adjacent houses which burn).

A new one should not be born with blood clots in its system, because then it would have the evil spell (dikgaba). That is not in keeping with the good order of things. A man-child or woman-child born with 'dikgaba' would perhaps be full of bitterness and vengeance. That is not to be. Such a man or a woman can either be a saviour or a devil whose heart would bleed for the nation.

Boitumelo's head was lowered and he could only see his feet keeping the rhythm of the other feet. His mind was full of a maze of mixed thoughts. . . . He mumbled to himself. . . .

. . . So it goes for those caught in the deadly spider's web. You never know when its tentacles will come closing in on you. But . . . 'inxeba lendoda kalihlekwa' (a man must never laugh at another man's running sore). . . . 'U-hixo uhamba ngerei' (God moves in a circle). What is now happening to the children of the black skin is no shock. Our forefathers, the wise ones, divined it long long ago: that the beloved land would one day be invaded by others from distant lands far far away; that the battles against them would be lost and that the noble sons of the soil would be harnessed like oxen; that the traitors amongst them – the hares that hunt with the hounds – would carry the whips and drive them deep into the flesh of their own kith and kin.

What is this anyway? How can a person created by the gods be held captive and tied down by another man? By what law is it? Surely that cannot be. . . . I am warning you. You are the 'Induna-boy' today but the tables will turn – ' È, Imnci!' I swear by my ancestors. Every dog has its day. . . . 'Moja-pele o tswana le moja-morao!' . . . I would like to tell you that while I spit in your face but I cannot. Someone can say that I am not a man. A man must speak his mind and call a spade a spade, not a big spoon. With my hands tied down I cannot strike back.

Soon I shall have to say: 'Guilty my Lord!' and point with my two fingers into the sky, like a parrot which has been taught to utter only the words of the master. When you are already on the edge of the pit, it needs a simple nudge to tumble you over.

Dimomona, Dimomona moratiwa keagorata. . . . Beloved I love you. Your vision comes before my eyes good and clear. You are sad, my sweet one – sweeter than your name suggests. Your sweetness is like the 'house' of bees. I could keep sucking you . . . 'Ke go momona fogosenang bokhutlo' . . . over and over again. I suck you because I never have enough of you. I wanted to let you know that the gods had whispered into my ear while I was asleep. Yes, that you should carry the new one with great care. Be careful never to cry that the new life should not be born with gall in its veins. The new one will learn the tongues of the foreigners and be our saviour.

Dimomona, Dimomona. . . . Even as I lie down on this cold cement floor, I can 'see' you as I always saw you. In the early hours of the morning I would watch you as you wake up from the grass mat on the floor. I would watch your beautiful eyes which sparkle like those of the young 'leodi' (bird). Your voice, as you softly hum the lyrics inspired by the crow of the 'first' cock, would send trembling waves into my heart and I would close my eyes and listen. A king for a while, I would be, and enjoy the hard 'throne' – the floor – the familiar smell of the cow-dung which you have spread on it, reaching my nostrils.

Oh, Dimomona, how can I ever hope to touch you again? Here I now lie on the cold cement slab, only because my skin did not have the 'stamp'. Had I known I would have sewn the cursed book on to my flesh. . . . I lie awake all night and think only of you.

On the Potato Farm. . . .

Dimomona, Dimomona, my back is aching and the sides of my ribs feel like cow-hide stretched to the limit. Anytime now, my chest will rupture from the whip-lash. The impact will perhaps cast me into the deep furrows I am digging with my bare hands and my finger-tips searching for the potatoes. In the deep trenches I shall be bleeding for you – from inside and outside. I am sad that I am not with you when you need me most. That I am not there to turn the handle of the 'Pits le Draai' (the pit and the handle). And to carry the pail of water from the well.

Oh, but for this venomous whip, striking right into my very bones. The loud wail of my fellow-sufferers when the white strikers look away and sit in the shade to watch. My pain is momentarily eased by the song of hope which keeps ringing back from within me:

'Abelungu ng'o-Dam, ng'o-Dam!
Abelungu ng'o-Dam, ng'o-Dam!
Amsen'e Ndun', eNdun'
Amasende. Ndun' eNdun!'

I curse . . . yes . . . the 'induna's' damned balls!

Oh Dimomona . . . who will provide for her now in this everyone-for-himself and God-for-us-all world of the white man where people seem to have lost their own good ways? Is God really for us too? Boitumelo wondered.

The weekly pay of two pounds and ten shillings was what he brought, neatly wrapped in a brown envelope, for their upkeep. He could still see how she always cupped her hands and bowed in her womanly fashion to denote her gratitude when he gave her the envelope. For the ancestors had given her a man who would go and toil and bring home the daily bread. What else could a good woman ask for? Surely her life was complete. Was it not a brave man's duty to walk in front and face the foe for his woman and kind? To absorb the impact from the kicks of the white man's boot? Boitumelo would surely be a dead man, dead inside to push his woman into the fire – into the kraals of the beasts!

It was in the early hours of the morning. Dimomona raised her eyes and looked at the treasured bicycle with its two carriers – one in front and one at the back. It was still there thank God. The police had not gone into the room during the morning of the raid. They, too, would have wondered how a mere black 'boy' could come to possess such a treasure. Dimomona remembered how Boitumelo always parked it inside the house except when he was polishing it. He would protect it with his own life, just like he would fight for his woman; but even more so because it was his white boss's property.

She would have to report Boitumelo's arrest to the big boss in town; and the boss would have to know that the bicycle was still safe. Yes, she knew what she would do. . . . In the extended family, who was more reliable than Mmane Liesbet? She was always the best aunt in the whole world. One could always count on her. A man would not be able to resist the temptation to ride the bicycle and show off his rare fortune. Mmane Liesbet would lock the door and sit in the room to guard the boss's bicycle. Or she would sit at the threshold, basking in the sun, with the bicycle safely 'tucked' away in the corner of the room behind her.

There was no problem going to the boss's place on a Sunday. It was a most convenient day because he was a Jew and he did not go to the Christian churches. Boitumelo used to spend hours speaking about his boss's likes and dislikes. It was always good to know everything about the boss. That way, you were always on the right side with him. It was also convenient for Dimomona because on Sunday mornings there were not so many cars moving in the roads, and the big city of Johannesburg was quiet. According to Boitumelo's advice, the big boss ('Base waka' like he so frequently and so fondly referred to him) was resting on Sunday mornings. Sunday was his resting day. He needed all that rest because he was a busy man. It was also best to go in the morning because in the afternoon he would be playing bowls in the Crown Mines Bowling Club with other big bosses who owned big businesses. She would walk the whole distance into town because as a country lass, she was accustomed to walking and, besides, she never felt comfortable in the buses. They banged and raced all the way and that was no good for her unborn child. A woman with a young one inside should be careful at all times. Accidents were known to happen even in the buses. If it had not been for the valuable bicycle she would not move too far from home because her 'time' was in fact near. She was in the last weeks of her pregnancy.

Dimomona trod carefully and quietly along the wide, beautiful Emmarentia Road, occasionally casting a stolen glance at the handsome mansions on either side of the street. The aroma from the flowers in the well kept gardens hit her nostrils and she knew that she would have to read the numbers carefully and not knock on the wrong gate. Boitumelo used to lecture to her about what was accepted as good behaviour for black people who enter the big luxurious suburbs of Johannesburg which he knew well and he hurried through daily delivering milk.

Boitumelo had also told her about the bell at the gate. She checked again and again to make certain that the big house with the towering palm trees and the big blooming luscious garden was that of Boitumelo's boss. She thought of the bell and stood at the gate, her eyes fixed on the dark brown knob. She hesitated and wished that the bell would put itself automatically into operation. She wondered how much pressure she would have to use to announce her presence without disturbing the boss and his wife.

Dimomona deliberately avoided the big front gate and moved towards the small one to the left which Boitumelo said was always used by black people. She stepped forward, aimed her trembling forefinger at the knob and pressed lightly. When she heard the shrill ring resounding inside, her heart missed a beat. She held on to the frills of the shawl hanging over her shoulders in order to summon enough courage. She took three paces backwards and stood on the pavement. She waited with bated breath. Two black guard dogs must have been disturbed because they immediately came charging towards the high fence. They hung over the wrought-iron gate, peeping and barking angrily. They were trained never to tolerate a strange black face especially, Boitumelo had told her. The sight of the hungry-looking hounds alone made Dimomona shudder with fright. They snarled furiously, their tongues hanging and flapping like pink flags held in position by long shining pointed canines, ready to tear at any prey. She stood cold and motionless, waiting.

The boss and his wife listened. The knock was unmistakably from the gate leading to the servants' quarters. The ringing of the bell by 'boys' and 'girls' so early in the morning was quite annoying. There was always the possibility that they wanted some money. What was it this time, they wondered . . . some uncle's cousin's brother dead or something? There never seemed to be an end to the fathers, uncles, brothers, aunts, sisters and mothers that these black people had. The boss and his wife had already lost count of the many occasions he had had to assist with an advance. But Boitumelo was more than a good 'baas-boy'. He was an asset to the company, although the boss never told him. That would not be good for the 'boy's' character and good behaviour. It was enough for him to know that he was trusted but not indispensible.

Jim, the house-boy, came hurriedly towards the small

gate. He took one look at the black woman with the shawl over her shoulders but could not recognise her. He enquired what the purpose of her 'visit' must be, speaking obviously impatiently. Whatever had made the woman wander to the 'doorstep' of his master would have to be dismissed with as little fuss as possible. The boss's wife had given instructions.

Dimomona explained about her predicament and the fact that the matter of the boss's valuable bicycle would have to be resolved. That Boitumelo – the chief so-called milk-boy – had been arrested for not having his pass on him. Jim shook his head, fearing for what would happen to the boss's bicycle in the township if it came to be known that Boitumelo was in gaol. He scampered back into the big house still shaking his head.

Jim knocked softly at the door of his master's bedroom. In response to the boss's instructions behind the closed door, he stammered the sad message of the boss's bicycle. He waited quietly, servile and obedient, listening to the boss's final resolve.

'Yes, baas; yes, baas,' he kept repeating, his knees shaking and the kitchen cloth hanging over his shoulder.

'Tell baas-boy milk-boy's woman I'll send someone to fetch the bicycle tomorrow quick. Do you hear that, Jim?'

'Yes, baas; yes, baas,' Jim replied.

With a forced smile on his face, Jim scuttled away squirming, his back hunched like a frightened squirrel. He was thinking of how well the boss had received the shocking news of his valuable bicycle in that township.

Inside the bedroom, the Missus repeated, 'Arrested! For a pass? One would expect them to know by now that they must always have their passes *on them*. It is always the same story. . . . Amazing how they always manage to get themselves into gaol!'

It was still very early and the street lamps lit the well. Dimomona tied a light shawl round her very distended waistline and let it fall gracefully over her dress like an additional skirt. There was not a drop of water left in the three tins lined on the cupboard at the corner. She decided to go and draw some.

She walked confidently towards the well telling herself that she would demonstrate to her neighbours that she, too, could be just as good as they were at operating the pit. The kindly woman next-door had always taken it upon herself to draw water for Dimomona ever since Boitumelo got arrested. Most of the women from the remote parts of the country were not accustomed to the way of life in the towns and they had to learn to use the pit and handle. 'Motho ke ke motho ka batho ba bangwe' (a person is a person because of other people), so the saying went and in the 1930s, even in a big city like Johannesburg, people still respected the customs. But Dimomona felt that a little bit of independence would not hurt anyone. She would only draw one pail, she reasoned. In the village from which she had come, she thought, one would not have given the simple act of drawing water a second thought at all. There were natural springs all over and the easy chore would have been accomplished in no time. But now this. . . .

She let the three or four early-morning workers go past before she stepped on the circular concrete platform and carefully removed the rectangular zinc lid, avoiding casting a glance into the yawning dark opening. She put the lid aside and turned the handle to lower the bucket. A few feet down, the pail began to swing from side to side, knocking against the walls of the well as it swayed. The rickety worn ends of the beams could not balance the structure rigidly and the woman had to lean forward to steady the rope in order to stop it from swinging like a pendulum. She smiled when she felt that the bucket had reached the level of the water down below and she waited as she felt it sink into the water. The rope tightened. That meant that the receptacle was now full. The task had been accomplished and all that remained was to turn the handle and pull the bucket up. She continued to wind the rope as gracefully as she could, just the way the other women did. But now, the side-to-side rocking began. It gradually became more and more vigorous, making the rope move more and more towards the walls. Dimomona's head swirled as she bent forward to reach for the rope in an attempt to steady it. She blinked nervously as she saw the dark bottomless pit below. She felt dizzy. Her foot slipped over the cement floor under her and in an instant, her balance was disturbed and she lost her grip on the handle while at the same time she tried to grasp harder on the rope with her other hand. The free handle, pulled down heavily by the weight of the full pail, turned swiftly back in an anti-clockwise direction. There was a loud whizzing sound and the 'load' sank fast into the deep well.

As if sucked in by some mysterious force, the half-dazed young expectant woman held tightly on the rope with both her hands. The yawning pit had swallowed her, and her desperate cries were audible to everyone behind the closed doors. The bewildered residents were quickly roused from their early morning slumber, and they immediately ran out, joining the stunned workers to form a circle round the concrete platform. There were wailing yells from the women as everyone gazed helplessly and expectantly into the pit.

'Inchu-u-u!' came the soft muffled sound as if from a long distance away. 'Dimomona-a-a!' one of the women shouted back. She asked anxiously, 'Awaphela?' (Are you alive?) The wailing and the screaming stopped suddenly, everyone straining his or her ears to hear what the answer would be. Some even feared that the 'Ichu!' could have been her last gasp for breath before the dear woman lost her life. They strained their ears and held their breath.

'Ke a phela!' the trembling voice assured them. It was unbelievable. The listeners heaved a sigh of relief. Dimomona was indeed alive.

The drama could have ended tragically; instead it ended happily. The young woman had cheated death by a stroke of luck. Indeed her ancestors had snatched her from the jaws of a lion. 'Only a miracle, straight from Dimomona's long-departed forefathers, could have saved her in that manner!' an old woman remarked thankfully, and everyone nodded their heads in full agreement. Some of the women had already collected blankets from their beds to wrap the 'miracle mother', rub her dry and nurse her.

In two shakes of a duck's tail, a flat rectangular wooden bench with two strong chains securely attached at both ends was supplied by Ah Chin, the Chinaman of the nearby grocery shop. Dimomona was advised to sit on it and hold on to the chains like a child on a swing. Two very strong men stood over the hole on either side and pulled the smiling woman up to safety. The water inside the pit had only reached her waistline, she said. Apart from shock and a few bruises sustained on her knees and elbows, she was as sound as a fiddle, she assured everybody with a sigh.

Exactly twenty-four hours later, Dimomona gave birth to – not one, but two bonny sons. In spite of what had befallen the young couple, the gods had offered them more than a reward. There was something

wonderful to meet poor Boitumelo when the time came
for his release from prison.

Mmane Liesbet announced proudly that the names of
the two boys would be 'Pits le Draai' (Pit and Handle)
and everyone agreed that the names were fitting to make
everyone remember always the miracle from the ancestors. The boys' clan names would be Kgomotso le
Mogomotsi (Consolation and Consoler).

The dear old lady came to live with Dimomona and
the twin boys permanently, until Boitumelo came back.
Appeals to Boitumelo's boss for financial help had been
fruitless. He made Dimomona understand that there
was no law which forced him to offer anything, that in
fact the law was very unsympathetic towards careless
'boys' who got themselves arrested. Nevertheless what
he could give her, 'for only three months at the most',
was a weekly pay of half what her husband earned.
From the money, Dimomona had to pay rent and buy
five pounds of maize meal. The open veld between
Sophiatown and Westdene would supply 'morogo' –
a succulent green plant which would be 'seshebo' –
something to go with the mealie-pap. Mmane Liesbet
would go daily to pick 'morogo' so that the boys would
suck milk coming from their mother's breasts.

The guard had unexpectedly announced that four of the
Cell D prisoners would be discharged that week, and
that Boitumelo was to be one of them. He could hardly
believe that he would really be free to go home after
digging potatoes with his bare hands for four whole
months on the Bethal farms. Any day now, the heavy
prison gates would be opened and they would be herded
out. He lay in the sun wondering what it would be like
to see Dimomona again. He counted the months on his
fingers and thought that her 'time' must have passed;

that she might be the mother of yet another one of his own, son or daughter.

The slanting sharp rays of the sun penetrated the clouds which were moving swiftly across the part of the sky which was visible to Boitumelo from the narrow enclosed prison yard. He lay on his stiff back still feeling the awkwardness caused by the thick scars where the whips and the 'sjamboks' of the prison overseers had mercilessly cut through his flesh. It was Sunday afternoon after the miserable-looking priest from the nearby Bethal village had delivered the sermon. Boitumelo remembered how his words of warning and pleas for spiritual revival had sounded like empty meaningless pronouncements; words, just utterances. The 'man of God' wore a shabby black tweed jacket with a partially bleached bib (which must have been black in its earlier days) and a yellowing rim of plastic collar just below his chin. He remembered that the preacher's neck had been too thin for the collar. The priest read passages from the Holy Bible and he spoke of the need to turn away from sin and the value of repentance because, he said, the coming of the Lord was near. The Son of God, he reminded them, had come to redeem all sinners and had been crucified so that those who were sinners like him (Boitumelo and the others) and the others in bondage should be saved. He asked them to come forward, kneel at the feet of the Lord and be born again. Boitumelo remembered that he in fact listened to the preacher, not because his words meant anything much, but because he had pitied the man. Boitumelo wondered whether he was being paid to deliver the sermon. 'Blessed are the meek for they shall inherit the earth,' the preacher emphasised sternly.

As Boitumelo lay on the floor, he ran his hands over the rough scars on his skin – his chest, his arms, his legs. The scars were thick, itchy and bloated. He knew that they were not 'normal' scars, that it would be long before they were completely healed and free of the pus in them. He wondered whether the 'man of God' should not rather have preached to the prison warders, the police, and all the law makers. He thought that it was *they* who needed to be 'saved' and not him and the poor struggling harnessed prisoners, many of whom had in fact committed no sin. 'What have I done to deserve all the punishment?' he asked himself again and again, looking at his blistered, blobbed finger-tips. As far as Boitumelo could see, the white people in this land were virtually the 'inheritors of the earth', and they could never be said to be 'meek'. With their guns, their shining bandoliers over their bulky chests, their mighty stallions strutted around proudly while those like him cowered and floundered uncertainly and were afraid when the 'inheritors' appeared.

It was Tuesday evening. The little girls hopping and skipping on the pavement in Good Street, Sophiatown, hardly noticed the limping figure in creased tattered clothes who entered the yard. It was not unusual to see such people moving seemingly aimlessly around the township. Some were people with nowhere to sleep who moved from the rubbish heaps to the gutters where they sought shelter at night, and others were so-called vagrants forever hiding from the police.

The cluster of people warming themselves round a brazier only cast a casual look at Boitumelo as he passed without greeting. It was evening and many people – mainly menfolk returning from work – had been passing and entering various rooms in the big yard where they usually went to enjoy their African brew before retiring to their homes.

Boitumelo knocked on the door of the fifth room from the gate. It was his room, his home. It was a relief to be home at last. He had had a tiresome uncomfortable journey in the train carriage normally set aside for transporting oxen. The prison guards had announced that they were free men and they were loaded in one of the carriages from Bethal Station. Whether the men would find their way back to their homes was no concern of the prison officials.

Mmane Liesbet opened the door and exclaimed, 'Jo oee!' She stepped back, startled with fright. She could not believe her own eyes. Was it really Boitumelo she was seeing there or was it only the ghost of her nephew? She was stunned. Dimomona stood up sharply and looked over Mmane Liesbet's shoulder. The dark face with unkempt hair and overgrown beard was indeed that of her husband. She was carrying a baby in her arms.

'Ao, Boitumelo!' was all she could stammer in her confusion. She put the baby on the floor-bed and moved to the door to welcome her husband. An apparition would not be seen by two pairs of eyes at the same time. Boitumelo was indeed home; she and Mmane Liesbet were not dreaming. Mmane Liesbet stood at the entrance clapping her hands and announcing loudly that her 'long-lost' nephew had returned from the house of damnation.

Dimomona's Kgomotso and Mogomotsi were identical twins. It only meant one thing . . . that he, Boitumelo, had been blest with a pair of healthy sons. A son was always an assurance that the clan would multiply. Kgope's name would live for ever. Boitumelo was more than thankful. He had always wondered whether Dimomona would be able to pull through her difficult 'waiting' without his nearness and support. He had feared the worst. The ancestors were indeed with them; the twins' nicknames (Pits le Draai) and the survival story behind the circumstances of their birth were proof of the greatness of He who created all.

The news of Boitumelo's unexpected arrival spread through all the nearby streets like wild fire. Because of his boss's shimmering bicycle, Boitumelo had always been a well-known Sophiatown resident.

Rakgokong, Boitumelo's best friend, was one of the first people to come and 'see for himself the amazing deeds of the ancestors'. As soon as he entered the room and saw his friend, he removed his hat and knelt down on one knee rather than sit on a chair. The gods had to be thanked and what better way was there but to kneel down? Not many people who had been condemned to serve prison terms had come back alive. Many of them had had their bodies thrust into the furrows of the potato fields. 'Badimo ga ba tlholwe ke sepe!' (the departed ones are almighty).

What remained was for him to come later to supervise personally the cleansing of Boitumelo so that the bad spirits (senyama) that must have followed him from gaol should be removed. A male person from Boitumelo's mother's people would have to come and carry out the 'sacred' ritual. Boitumelo would have to be immersed in a tub of warm water in which the powerful leaves of the cactus plant had been soaked. The evil spirits would have to be chased away by covering his head in smoke from the potions of his clan. His head and beard would have to be shaved clean and his limbs would have to be rubbed with healing ointments until they regained their strength. His whole body, which was riddled with bad unhealed scars, would have to be treated with the right weeds. A lamb would have to be slaughtered.

But if the friends and many well-wishers of the Kgopes had known what lay in store for Boitumelo and his family, they would not have had visions of a good ending to what had happened. How many a beautiful dream has been shattered at the thresholds of the white masters? Many have always sighed that the tears that have run from the eyes of the sons and daughters of the soil could flood the oceans.

On the following morning, Boitumelo went to the firm.

One look at his former chief so-called delivery boy convinced the boss that Boitumelo would never be able to do any work for him.

'You have paid dearly for your carelessness, my boy!' the boss said, pointing an accusing finger at him. He reminded him that in his business he could only employ someone who was healthy and strong. He added disdainfully, 'There's nothing I can do for you now. I'll have to sign you off and you'll have to go back to the farms. You'll never be able to pedal the bicycle again.'

Boitumelo returned home and announced sadly, 'Base waka onkobile' (My boss has chased me away).

Mmane Liesbet and Dimomona stared at him wide-eyed with disbelief. He concluded, 'Now that I am a sick man, he does not want me. He has signed my pass off. We shall have to go.'

The sad story was soon relayed to every room in the yard, and to friends and relatives in other yards. Some came to see Boitumelo and to let his family know that they sympathised. That whole day, the Kgopes welcomed a continuous retinue of sad-faced neighbours, most of them women with shawls hung over their shoulders as a sign of respect. What had happened to Boitumelo and his family was something that could befall anyone, they kept repeating. Some added that it was strange how God gives with one hand and takes with the other. The ancestors had spared Dimomona's life and had given them Kgomotso and Mogomotsi, Rakgokong remarked with tears flooding his eyes. He summed it all up by adding, 'But now, a piece of paper called a pass has reduced him to nothing!'

From money got by selling their table, the bench and some utensils, they raised enough money to pay for their train fares from Johannesburg Station to Loskop.

Two days later Mmane Liesbet spread an old blanket on the floor and Dimomona packed all their clothes on it. It would serve as a portmanteau. They tied the bundle securely with thick twine to make it easier for Dimomona to balance it on her head. She and Mmane Liesbet would each carry one twin on her back and Boitumelo would hobble alongside. It was a long way from Loskop Station to Mabieskraal and the three would have to rest at intervals along the way.

'Go in Peace, Tobias Son of Opperman'

Jessie sat on the chair in the small kitchen. She was thinking. About five minutes had gone since Tobias, her husband, had disappeared into their bedroom. Would he be washing, she wondered? To her sluggish mind, it seemed like hours since he had shambled in that direction. 'Alone again,' she thought, 'I'm alone.' She dreaded the thought of being alone with only Tikie the cat and the old Big Ben clock on the old kitchen dresser over there, ticking away the seconds and the minutes, and the hours; endless hours of waiting. Waiting for someone to knock at the door.

She called out, her voice weak and shaky, 'Tobie, where are you?'

'In here,' her husband answered.

'What are you doing there for such a long time?'

Tobias did not answer. He was looking at his reflection on the piece of broken mirror on the rickety chest of drawers in the dimly lit bedroom, his shaky hands flapping the broad end of his neck-tie into the loop and pulling it down, adjusting it to hang over his sternum.

On such days there was only one thing to do. . . . Go . . . go anywhere; talk to people and not reflect on

what might have been or might not have been, if, if, if.
What had happened in their lives had happened. It was
part of the past which no one could bring back or alter.
It was one of those days again. Jessie was again in those
moods of hers. If only she could accept her lot, her
long protracted illness, and leave everything into the
hands of the Creator. . . . He swallowed, he almost
wished he could 'swallow' the thought. If *he*, Tobias,
ever tried to quote one verse from the Bible to Jessie –
just one verse – he would regret it for the whole day.
The dear woman seemed to have sunk deeper and deeper
(in the twelve long years of her infirmity) into a world
of despair and emptiness. Emptiness, nothingness. Even
the prayers Matlome and Mma-Matlome their close
friends came to comfort them with every week seemed
of late to have no meaning to her. She no longer derived
any strength from them. Matlome's words seemed to
leave his lips, hit Jessie's hard stolid face and then
bounce back to him without even reaching her ears. On
such occasions, she just stared into the air and she would
not utter a word of appreciation. At least whenever
Matlome quoted verses from the scriptures, Jessie's
stern face did not seem to recoil into a hard knot. She
would not even stammer bitterly: 'Don't come to me
again with those "holy" words Tobias son of
Opperman, please. I know you too well to take you
seriously . . . words, words, words. You always say
words you yourself do not mean, Tobiase.'

It was still early but Tobias felt tired already. He cast
a final look into the mirror before him, drawing back
slowly and murmuring to himself, 'Old age. You wake
up tired as if you never slept at all!'

He had woken up early to make fire in their 'Welcome
Dover' coal stove. He had also prepared their breakfast,
thin mealie-meal porridge as usual. As he moved

towards the kitchen, he felt happy about his accomplishments. . . . The kitchen was warm and cosy. The pot of porridge was simmering slowly. He was thinking and his lips were moving, whispering the thoughts as they occurred to him. 'I'll have to mix the powdered milk and make tea for both of us. . . . I must not forget to give Jessie the tablets for her arthritis,' he mumbled almost loudly and slouched back into their bedroom. At that moment, he wished that Nakedi, his brother's twelve-year-old great-grand-daughter, was there to go on errands. He was wondering when the schools would reopen. The school holidays seem to be so much longer nowadays, he thought regretfully. It was so thoughtful of their great-grand-nephew and niece to have 'offered' little Nakedi to stay with them to send around the house and to the shops. Now he would have to do everything himself until she returned from visiting her parents.

Tobias lumbered slowly back to the kitchen with the vial containing the pills for his wife. He looked at her, putting them on the table next to her, and advised, 'Don't forget to take your tablets, Jessie, I'll . . .'

'What's the use of taking them; they never work anyway,' Jessie cut in sharply. She turned her head and looked at Tobias and asked, 'How shall I forget them? You'll be here to. . . . You are not going away and leaving me alone again are you?' She nodded slowly, knowingly, added, 'Oh yes. Clean shirt, a suit, neck-tie and everything. You are ready to go again. You're so keen, you never even looked to see if your shirt is not inside-out!'

Tobias's hand moved immediately and unsteadily towards his neck. He had not yet buttoned his shirt and he had not noticed the mistake. 'Oh, I didn't notice.'

He shook his head. 'Old age,' he thought, 'you never

seem to do things right. And all the time you try *so*
hard.' He looked at Jessie again and added, 'Shall I give
you your porridge now? I have to go. Will you manage?
I'll put everything next to you on the table – the bowl
of porridge, the spoon, the soup and the sliced bread.
Also sugar and the salt from the clinic. We don't have
any more jam. Are you listening, Jessie?'

Jessie did not reply. She was thinking how she hated
the very mention of *that* 'clinic' salt. It tasted more like
Epsom salt than salt! She looked ahead of her at nothing
in particular. The aches in her legs were just beginning
to intensify. She sat still, feeling the painful twinge come
and go, come and go. The pains were spreading through
her joints and piercing mercilessly all over her body like
spikes of fire. That look of utter helplessness had come
over her face again. She shut her eyes and said nothing.

A few minutes later, Tobias walked into the bedroom
and picked up his hat and his umbrella. 'I'll be back,
Jessie,' he mumbled as he went past her. He shut the
door quietly behind him and walked slowly towards the
gate.

With her eyes still closed, Jessie 'spoke' to Tobias
who she knew was not in the house and would not hear
her.

'Ikele ka kagiso Tobiase Mor'waga Opperman.
Balimo ba me ba tla sala le nna' (Go well Tobias son of
Opperman. My ancestors will remain with me). The
white man's language you speak, their ways which you
learnt since you were born and their name that you
carry with you have only meant misery for me. When
I married you, I thought that you would make me
happy because you are not what they call "die kraal-
kaffer". Like them (whites), you have no feelings for
fellow human beings. You just have no "marrow".
You're lost.'

In the street, Tobias was thinking. Although he did not realise it, he was speaking loudly as if Jessie was still sitting next to him. He did not look back. He just kept walking and walking and soliloquising. . . . He knew deep down, however, that he would never say what was in his mind to his wife. . . . 'I know what will happen if I stay next to you when you are like that, Jessie. You will be blaming me for everything that went wrong in our life; everything that was not gratifying and pleasant. You'll be blaming me for everything as if *I* make all the laws between human beings. Between men and women; the rich and the poor; white people and black people. What am I anyway? Just a struggling old man. . . . If during my youth I made mistakes, can they be worse than anybody else's? Like everybody else, I was only trying hard to eke out a living in a difficult world.'

Tobias knew that he would never say all those things to his ailing wife. As you grow older, you learn the wisdom in the words 'ho boloka khotso' in a marriage. You begin to appreciate how important it is. You come to realise that there are younger people around you who have to be assisted along the hazardous path of life shared, of marriage. Just like his father used to say to him and his sisters and brothers – all dead and buried now. 'Trou is nie perde-koop nie,' he would repeat again and again. The truth in those words sank deeper and deeper as he grew older and you have to pass on words of advice to your descendants and the sons and daughters of those you live with. He remembered the tumultuous early years of their marriage when they were still living in a one-room tin shack in S'deke-deke near Westbury Station long long ago. 'Jarelanang mef-okolo bana ba ka.' An old Mosotho neighbour, old-man Nong, would pound on their door and enter without being asked to do so in an attempt to prevent what he thought would be a bloody duel of young people who had not learnt how to 'carry the cross'. 'Bolokang khotso bana ba ka! Jarelanang mefokolo,' the old man would say, stepping in between him and Jessie. (Do preserve peace my children. Bear with each other's weaknesses.) He could not remember how many times old-man Nong had stepped in, raising his hands high, reciting the words until they sounded like a commandment. He would then put his hands on Tobias's shoulder, pleading with him to sit down and 'cool off'. 'Sit down my child; do not raise your voice. A woman is a woman; you cannot compete with her tongue. Keep quiet or leave her and go elsewhere; when you return, she will have forgotten.'

It was a long time ago and they had come to know one another through the years. Their quarrels had gradually ceased to be noisy and stormy because they had learnt – painfully – 'ho boloka khotso'. Or was it because he *had* finally come to know that there was no point in trying to compete with a woman's tongue?

Tobias had automatically walked in the direction of his old friend Matlome's house like his feet were drawn to it by an invisible magnet. He stopped opposite the house and hesitated for a while. He decided not to go in. It was still too early to pay anyone a visit and besides he was still too irritated and upset to speak to anyone. And Mma-Matlome was a very observant old woman who seemed always to see through people. She always seemed to be examining people's faces for any hidden traces of uneasiness. She was like a specialist who was an expert in diagnosing 'maladies' associated with discontent, remorse or indignation. Tobias hurried away from the spot before anyone noticed his procrastination.

Nobody seemed to care. Everyone went past him, obviously hurrying to wherever they were going. Who cares about an old man when there are more urgent matters to see to anyway, he thought, thankful that no one who knew him was near enough to notice his sadness and perhaps ask questions. Only the kids who were kicking the ball in the street saw him. They too were more concerned with the ball than with him. They were dodging the familiar figure of old Oupa Tobias carrying the umbrella and the walking stick, always mumbling to himself. To them, it was fun to watch him as they kicked the ball around him; to look into his 'unseeing' eyes without paying attention to his muttering.

In the open space between Zone 9 and Zone 10 Meadowlands, he was still thinking loudly, 'speaking' to Jessie and listening to his own voice without making any effort to lower it. There was nobody in sight and he was grateful. . . .

'Even if I had tried to explain to you, you would have gone on and on accusing me of not caring. You would have told me again that all I cared about was *other* people – outside our house. What do you think would happen to us if I did not go round giving comfort to other old people and doing my part as a member of the Old Age Relief Committee in the church? The church gives us the milk powder, the soup powder, the beans, the mealie meal, the jam and the sugar. . . . Where would we get all that from if I did not help? Our pension money only manages to pay the rent; to buy coal, wood, the medicines, that's all. We can only buy meat two times a month, you know that. Unless some kind neighbour or relative brings us a packet now and again.

'It's your fault Jessie; it's all your fault. I used to tell you to stop doing the washing for the whites and you never listened to me. All those bundles and bundles you carried on your head to and from the white suburbs day after day, week after week, month after month. And now all the joints in your body have given in. Now you are crippled; an invalid. *Twelve years* and you are still helpless. . . . You are no longer the sprightly beautiful Jessie I married.'

Tobias shook his head at the thought and hot tears filled his eyes and he could not see the road ahead clearly. His boots kicked against the stones in the gravel path and he stumbled, holding tightly on to the stick in his hand. His limbs were tired and unsteady. He had been walking and walking without knowing where exactly he was going to. . . . Anywhere, anywhere away from the dark clouds which seemed forever to be engulfing his house. He thought of Nakedi. He continued to speak loudly, 'If only little Nakedi was there then there would be someone to speak to. To relate the stories of old Madlera and Thulandivivile, S'deke-deke and so on. To talk about the animals in the zoos and tell all sorts of tales about them. . . . The children, our children; why did they all go before us? When you give birth to children, you expect them to be there to close your eyes when you go. You do not expect them to leave you behind. . . . All three of them . . . all gone before us. Polio, meningitis, TB. . . . Why? If they were here, I would not have to bear the pain of watching Jessie alone . . . Jessie crawling like an insect before me; wasting away right there before my eyes. First a stroke, then arthritis and God-knows-what. . . . The children would help me carry Jessie from the chair to the toilet bowl; from the bed to the kitchen. . . . I have to "carry the cross" alone. My

shoulders, my arms, my legs – they're aching, tired. . . .
Jessie, Jessie, daughter of Magolebane, I am tired.'

In their little semi-detached house in Meadowlands,
Jessie had long finished eating her breakfast. It was now
long after lunchtime and she had not reached for her
bread and cold soup. She did not feel hungry at all. She
sat thinking and talking to herself, addressing Tobias
who was not there to listen. It did not matter to her
that he was not there to hear her. All she wanted to do
was to speak out her mind. She went on and on:
'Church work, church work . . . I know all about that,
Tobias. You forget that I know you. I did not stay with
you all my life for nothing. You are just a tramp – a
born tramp, Tobias. "I'm on the Committee; I must
have a suit." First it was the Boxing Board Committee,
then it was the Football League Committee. Then
followed the race-course and the "boys". You just had
to go somewhere. . . . Durban, Cape Town, Port Elizabeth, Messina, Walvis Bay, everywhere. . . . Suits,
suits, suits. A brown suit, a grey suit, a navy blue suit,
a black suit. . . . "What about the children Tobias? The
school fees, the school uniforms, the food, the children's
shoes, coats for winter – what about *them*?" I would
ask. The committees, the committees. They all came to
nothing, nothing. Then you would come home with
bloodshot eyes – drunk, after losing all your money at
the race track.

'And now it's the Old Age Relief Committee. . . .
Church work, church work. . . . Your field is becoming
smaller and smaller just like mine. Ever since the "street-
corner" kids stole your bicycle, your field is becoming
smaller and smaller and you still cannot see that. Mine
is even smaller because I can no longer walk outside and
greet people as they pass. I am now confined to the

little square where I am sitting. I have to crawl on my knees to go into the toilet and just that takes a whole hour. Exercises, the clinic nurse says; "Try to use your limbs, Ouma Jessie," she says, piercing my tired flabby muscles with the long needle like she were poking a harmless stick into a dead piece of leather. . . . And now I have to go again to the toilet and I don't know how I'll manage. The cat. Tikie, you can't help me either. If only I could send you to bring the bowl to me. . . . I have to crawl to that bowl over there. . . . What a cursed "blessing" these Meadowlands toilets are inside the house! The smell – so near the pots and the pans – kitchen smells, bedroom smells, lavatory smells all mingling together on my nostrils. It's just like Vundla (P.Q.) used to say at our weekly meetings in Thulandivile's Communal Hall: "The Boers want to take us to a Me-e-e-do (meadow). They want us to go to a place where 'Nxa ufun'uk'ye-bosh' " (when you want to go and shit) and you are sitting outside, you go *into* the house to do that!" And we used to think he was mad, and the idea would be repulsive and nauseating, and we would spit. Everything put next to each other like that. . . . Fit only for derelicts like ourselves. People who have been used and discarded; forgotten by the glittering world of gold sixteen miles away. . . . We have helped to build their skyscrapers and now we are only fit for the rubbish heap. They can now sit in their posh buildings and forget about us Tobias. . . . Now you have to hire a wheelbarrow and get a pair of strong youths to push it and take me to the superintendent's office every two months for us to collect our pension money because they will never give you *my* pension unless they *see* me. . . . That's what it has come to now Tobias. . . . And now you too have cast me away to face the end alone.'

The kitchen had gradually become darker and darker. Jessie wondered why Tobias had stayed away so late. It had started to rain and the dark clouds had made it look like it was late in the evening.

'Ouma! Ouma Jessie!' a child's voice called from outside the door. It sounded like it was coming nearer her. It was not easy to turn her head and see behind her. The muscles in her neck were stiff and it had been years since she could easily twist her neck-bones. It was typical of her type of illness, the doctor and the clinic nurses had said.

The child stopped as soon as he entered the little kitchen. He was surprised. Jessie was sitting on the floor, the cat cuddling on her dress between her knees. He stammered, 'Ouma, I've brought Oupa Tobias. . . . But, but why is Ouma sitting on the floor?'

He moved to face Jessie squarely, puzzled. The child's face was familiar but Jessie could not say exactly whose child he was. Just one of the kids in the neighbourhood. He was holding on to Tobias with his one hand and clasping the umbrella and the walking stick in the other. He did not wait for Ouma Jessie to reply, but explained because he could see that she was herself taken aback by what she was seeing. She tried to explain, her attention directed at Tobias. She drawled uncertainly, her tongue feeling heavy like it had suddenly become too big in her mouth, making it difficult for her to speak clearly.

'M-my s-stick, Tobias. . . . I tried to reach for it and it slipped and rolled away. I . . . I'm too tired. I could not reach it. It was only the cat Tikie and I. It was from the toilet over there. I could not get on to the chair without the stick. The . . . the cat could not give it to me. . . . I sat waiting for you to come and help me, Tobias. You've been gone for *so* long.'

Tobias did not speak. His eyes seemed to be staring at something ahead of him. His knees began to sag and he dropped down with a thud on the floor next to Jessie.

'Oupa!' the child screamed. He jumped and tried to pick up the old man who was now sprawling, spreading his arms outward with his face towards the corrugated iron roof and the rafters above.

'No, leave Oupa alone, my child! Go out and call somebody! A neighbour – anybody; go!'

Jessie could not mistake that look on Tobias's face. His head was just near her knees. She wished she could pick him up and put him on her lap. His eyes were still staring. She talked to the still form before her: 'You are surprised, Tobias. So am I. You have cheated me once more. You were always so strong and now you have gone before me. Why are you so cruel, Tobias? How I wish I were you, Tobias. You will no longer have to reach for the umbrella and the walking stick and trample the streets. . . . You have cheated me again. I always worked so hard for you and the children and all you can do is leave me alone. "Ikele ka kagiso Tobiase mor'wa Opperman . . . Jy het my vermors." (You have wasted me).

Jessie looked at the surprised expression on the face of her dead husband for a while, her mind failing to grasp clearly what was happening to her. Slowly her shaking hand moved towards his fixed eyelids and closed them.

Metamorphosis

The narrow streets tapered even more towards the west where the sunken sun had left a beautiful golden glow barely visible in the grey smog. Velani noticed the crimson ardour only because he – out of impulse – had decided to remain seated in his Volkswagen Golf. One never really noticed the setting sun's beauty in Soweto. He shut his eyes and tried to listen to the music from the car radio.

He was waiting. He looked around. His car was parked near the gate of house no. 2249. In this township of Mapetla there were no numbers on the doors. They had been erased with white paint. The houses were faceless, mute match-boxes, Velani thought, smiling. The 'comrades' had done a perfect job of it. It was amazing how these youths thought of everything to befuddle the system. If he had been a stranger and did not know his uncle's house, he would have been completely at a loss as to which one of the rows of similar match-boxes on either side of the dusty road it was. His wife, Mavis, a district nurse, had often spoken of developments in and around the townships but he had never really taken everything seriously. All she said had been just a lot of 'women-talk'. Even at the 'spot' which he frequented, the 'Suzzie's Haunt', people had alluded casually to 'incidents' but he always thought there were more serious matters a man could think of. He recalled that Mavis had once said that it was important for the struggle that we be one thing, no one should be labelled 'good' or 'bad' by the authorities, that injury to the one must be injury to the next. 'After all,' they say, 'we are all black; we all belong to the soil. Besides, we are all oppressed. An attack on the one must be an attack on all.'

Velani tried to listen to the music but the kids in the street were excited. They were frolicking around, jumping and chasing one another. He looked through the window and clicked his tongue loudly. He shut the window and closed his eyes. It was becoming dark and he was sitting there waiting for his mother – affectionately known as Aunt Tilly (for Matilda) – and his sister Tembi. He spoke to himself: 'Waiting. . . . "Ngisal-indile namanje" I'm still waiting even now. You always have to wait for "abantu bes'fazane", womenfolk. They never seem to get over what they are doing. It doesn't matter whether it's talking, washing their faces, exchanging greetings, even praying. . . . I bet they're on their knees right now, praying "Nkulunkul' olungile-e-e-eyo . . . Nkulunkul' olungile-e-eyo!" (merciful God. . . . merciful God!).' He shook his head vigorously. And this was Friday mind you, he thought regretfully; Friday, the day on which he and the 'MaGents' would normally be 'in conference', enjoying good music, chatting the night away over a c-o-o-l beer.

It was his own fault, Velani thought regretfully. What on earth had made him go via his mother's house anyway? Somehow his dear mother never seemed to hesitate to send him off on one errand or another. On this day, he had tried to dissuade her. He had emphasised, 'You know, Ma, that I never refuse to drive you to "U-Malume" (Uncle's place). But *today* . . . it's not safe to drive to Deep Soweto, surely you *know* that Ma. Moreover, travelling there with two "abantubes' fazane". . . . If you were *men*, yes: but "abantubes' fazane. . . .' He shook his head. . . . 'Hayi, hayi, hayi.'

To which his mother replied, 'But Velie, you rarely ever come except in the late hours. In fact, this time you're early. And you *know* that unless you drive me to U-Malume's place I can never hope to see him. Besides, I don't think I can have a good night's sleep when a message came this morning that your Uncle Bafana is very ill indeed. Who knows what can happen? Even *he* would rush here if he received news that I was on the brink of. . . .' She dared not mention 'Death', no: not her beloved brother Bafana. She had pleaded, 'Please my son, drive me there. Your sister Tembi can help me walk.'

Velani tried to drive his point home. He added, smiling, 'But you three are the ones. . . . Your daughter-in-law Mavis, your daughter Tembi and *you*, Ma. . . . You three are the ones always speaking about "ama-'necklace', 'a-Makabasa,' a-ma-'Comrades' yonke lento" and now. . . .'

His mother interjected, waving apologetically, 'Velie, Bafana is my own brother, my mother's and my father's only other living child. His end is near; I can feel it. You don't seem to realise that it's only the two of us left now. When he goes, I'll be left alone.'

Tembi, who had been busy in the bedroom, was now standing at the entrance to the dining-room, listening and smiling. She anticipated what Velani was going to say and the two were amused. He said, 'Why Ma always says "only the two of us are left" I don't know. Doesn't Ma also have another brother in Eldorado Park? What about *him*? Just the other day I passed at the coloured township with a friend of mine who wanted to have his car panel-beaten by Uncle Boetie – Uncle Mbuti to be correct. Isn't he also your very own mother's and father's son? Why do you always exclude him as if he doesn't exist?'

Aunt Tillie's two children were relieved that in spite of their mother's sadness, there was a smile on her face as she replied, 'You two know the answer to that one. I have told you on many occasions that it is because we all have to remember always to refer to him as Uncle Boetie McCabel and not Mbuti Mkhabela. He does not want to be exposed and known as "unyana ka Mkhabela" (son of Mkhabela). That, as you very well know, would take the bread out of his mouth. In this country, it is only the fairer ones who eat, don't you know?'

The three were now ready to go, Tembi following her brother on whose arm their mother was leaning. As she clung to the strong biceps of her son, Aunt Tillie felt safe and she moved slowly and confidently over the uneven bricks of the pathway leading to the 'Volksie'. When she was seated comfortably on the back seat, Velani took the travelling rug Tembi was holding and tucked it gently around his mother's knees. He smiled into his mother's face. It was a strong, stoic and steadfast face which, to both her children, never seemed to yield to the vicissitudes of life and the inevitable hazards of ageing.

The radio blared away and Velani listened and watched as the red arm on the car-watch ticked the seconds on and on. His boot tapped almost unconsciously to the rhythm of the song and he kept his eyes closed. When the music stopped, he opened his eyes and looked through the windscreen into the thick grey smog which competed with the dotted heaps of garbage, ash and rubbish of every description. The unsightly mounds formed a screen on the narrow end of the road where a short while ago he had watched the rosy hue of the setting sun. Velani clicked his tongue again and kept his eyes focussed on the faintly illuminated dashboard. The record had stopped. Velani wished that the rather too enthusiastic announcer would stop his remarks and let the bands play on without stopping. He stretched his arm, clicking his tongue once more. He reached for the dial-knob and moved the cord from so-called 'Radio Zulu' to so-called 'Radio Bophuthatswana'. He scoffed loudly, 'These howlers should be fired!'

On 'Radio Bop' a drumming thumping hit was playing and Velani smiled as he twisted his torso, rolling his eyes dreamily in sheer ecstasy. The boredom he had experienced a while ago seemed to wear away.

When Velani opened his eyes again, the sun had gone completely, leaving the sky dull and murky, with the thick smog hanging as if suspended in mid-air from some invisible 'frame'. He knew that no breeze would clear the dense menace.

It was quite dark outside in the street now, and the people kept passing. Their footsteps were more brisk. Velani could only just make out from their obscure silhouettes that they were men, women and children. He remembered that it was Friday, and on Friday night people hurry home to the safety of their match-boxes. Only the brave and daring ones remain. The footsteps were awkward and now and again Velani could hear a woman's voice groan, 'Ichu-u-u!' as she stumbled, apparently knocking her toes against a stone. The rocky

roads had been eroded by the rains into uneven foot-
paths and the jutting rocks were everywhere, merging
with the wire fences on what should have been pave-
ments but were now sloping irregular 'banks'.

There was a loud thud on the window and Velani
started. The knock was so close that it felt like it was
from inside his own head. The dark figures on both
sides of the car were peering eagerly. A quick glance
around made Velani realise at once that the car was in
fact completely surrounded by a number of youths.
Most of them were wearing 'ballaclavas' with brims
lowered over their eyebrows. Velani was shaken, but
something within him told him that there was no need
to fear, that he was not going to be intimidated because
he was not born yesterday. He switched off the radio
and asked furiously, 'What's the matter?'

There were several hard taps on all four side windows,
and impatient shouts of, 'Vula, bula, bula!'

'What is it?' Velani asked.

'Vula, vula! Open the window or we break all of
them!'

The youths meant business but Velani was no 'Mafi-
kizolo'. He would not give in to their demands. He
looked around and asked, 'Why?'

Some of them replied, 'We would like to borrow your
car. We have to attend a vigil of one of our boys who
was shot dead by the police in Emdeni. Are you going
to give us the car or not? Just open and let us in. You
can drive us there if you want. Open!'

'No; I won't!' Velani shouted back, determined to
hold his ground.

The car rocked uncomfortably on to one side and he
felt his stomach fold into a knot. His heart beat faster

and the sweat ran down his temples and forehead. There was an even louder chorus from outside: 'Open!'

This was real trouble. Had his ancestors turned their backs on *him*, Velani, who was never a coward? But even if he tried to fight the mob he would never overpower them. They were too many. They were wielding knives, sharp instruments and iron bars. He just could not understand it. The stark shocking reality of what he had up to then only imagined was happening to *him*; he, Velani, a 'clever' of Soweto. . . . No, it can't. Not to *him*. He shouted stubbornly, 'I won't open!'

Again the car rocked uneasily as if it were resting on foam; and his entrails felt like they were suspended in a jelly-like fluid. He felt sick. What was he to do? According to what he knew, from what he heard from his wife, his mother and his sister, in fact all those who made it their business to attend the people's meetings, no right-thinking 'comrades' would do that, not to *him*. Wasn't he a well known 'clever' with all the power of a real man? He *had* to be a man. He challenged them, 'Do what you like; I won't open!'

Crash! came the violent sound. Velani looked back and saw that the rear window was now a mosaic of broken glass. In the centre was a gaping hole as big as the fist of a full-grown man, where a heavy steel bar had landed. The bloodshot vicious eyeballs of one of the assailants peered at him through the window next to him. He pointed a clenched menacing fist at Velani, threatening, 'Sizak'nyova thi-ina, grootman uyezwa? Uyacu-u-uga ne?'

A whistle . . . a whistle. . . . If only he could sound a loud SOS. Call someone, everybody, anybody to come to his assistance. Had his mother, his sister, his wife, all those who attended 'the people's meetings' not warned him to carry a whistle wherever he went? And

that he thought was only 'woman talk' . . . sheer
cowardice. But now he had to act. His life, his beloved
'Volksie'. . . . All these thoughts raced through his
mind in a flash. He *had* to do something. In that state
of uncertainty and fear, his 'manly' thumb groped for
the hooter and pressed it down . . . hard. The car came
down with a clamorous bang, and only then did he
realise that the youths were going to turn it over.

His call had aroused people inside nearby houses.
Doors and windows were flung open. Tembi was the
first one to emerge, from his uncle's home nearby. Her
shrill voice pierced through the dark night, making an
urgent appeal for help. Whistle-sounds from windows
all around permeated through the thick smog, sending
alarm signals in all directions. Velani knew that it was
the women – mothers, sisters, wives – who were
blowing the whistles. At that moment he seemed to hear
the voice of his wife resound the resolve of the people
in distress: 'The system does not care. All they want is
to exploit us. They will never go out of their way to
protect us. Stand together and fight as one. They are
guarding the borders and hunting for so-called terrorists
like you look for a needle in a haystack. Blackman
you're on your own. Only *you* can root out the evil in
your midst and its hired lackeys who are only there
to confuse the people; to distract them from the real
enemy. . . .' It was bad for the marauding youths.
Velani watched them still in a state of complete paralysis
and shock. They sauntered away in all directions, some
dropping their weapons as they scaled over the dilapi-
dated fences into the adjoining streets and vanished.

'Cowards!' Velani cursed, spitting through the
window which he had now opened to assure the
converging people that *he*, Velani, was safe and sound.

'Soweto is a jungle. I don't know what you want there. You should come to Eldorado Park. We coloureds here are safe!'

Velani remembered the words of hope his uncle had often whispered to him when he paid him a 'business' call. None of Boetie McCabel's neighbours and friends had ever suspected that he was in fact an African who, according to the South African divide-and-rule laws, should have been in Soweto. Who could have known that he was Mbuti Mkhabela? On his not-so-frequent 'visits' to his uncle in Eldorado Park, Velani had been like all McCabel's African customers from Soweto. From a struggling start, Uncle Boetie's panel-beaters had flourished over the twenty-five years in that township. Only his fair-skinned wife had known the secret and she had vowed to keep it from anyone's 'prying' ears.

Very often now, while he lay in bed thinking, Velani became increasingly uneasy. All right, he had fitted on a new rear window to his 'Volksie'. . . . But what of the future? He was a traveller and often he did not sleep at home. The fences surrounding his house were not so good either. It would cost a fortune to erect good ones. The people were not paying rent. To do that would be to risk getting a 'necklace'. The signs were all over . . . 'YOU PAY, WE BURN'. Who would risk that? Perhaps it was a good thing to leave Soweto and go to Eldorado Park after all.

Once while he lay awake in bed with his mind besieged by these thoughts, he patted his wife Mavis's shoulder gently to make a suggestion to her. She had just fallen asleep lightly. She grunted, 'Hm?' Her eyelids already heavy, she asked, 'What's the matter?'

At least Mavis was willing to listen, Velani thought, his mind already excited by what he had to tell her.

86

He asked, 'What if we pack up everything and go to Eldorado, May?'

Mavis was now fully awake. She replied, 'Velie, are you dreaming? Eldorado is somewhere in North America. Where have you ever heard of someone leaving Soweto to go and live so far away . . . even if one were crazy enough to think he or she could afford the plane ticket, let alone get a passport from the Boers?'

Velani answered anxiously, 'No. I mean the Eldorado next to "us"; next to Soweto, on the other side of Kliptown, May, please. Things are so difficult for us here now. Look, the car, the house, everything.'

'Heyi wena; are you crazy, what's wrong with you anyway? Why do you think you can run away from the struggle?'

Mavis shook her head in disbelief. Somehow she felt grateful. 'At least he is worried,' she said to herself. That silly suggestion he had made meant that he was restless. How long had she wished that Velani would stop 'floating around' in a cloud of self-deception and concern himself with what was happening? He would never even listen to what she had to say whenever she came from 'the people's' meetings. She sighed, 'The struggle is everywhere, Velie.'

'But the people in Eldorado lead normal lives. They pay rent, electricity bills and water. Their houses still have the numbers. Everything is going on smoothly.'

'So you think if you do that – run away to Eldorado – you'll be safe? OK, you want a house with a number so that the police, the army, the council messengers can spot you easily. You want to eat, sleep and drink in their "safe" hands. . . . What about those who cannot run away? Do you think you can build an island of comfort and safety around you when everyone else is oppressed? Not even the Boers still think they can.'

But Velani's coloured uncle's voice haunted him, and the harder he tried to forget it now of late, the more it goaded him: 'Leave that Soweto and come to Eldorado. The Immigration Control Laws, the 101 (a)s, (b)s, (c)s are all suspended.* They are scrapped for good. You can live anywhere you like now. Save your neck and your property. Come to our coloured township. Come to Eldorado.'

Velani could not remember when he finally fell asleep.

Whether Velani's ancestors had turned their backs towards him, he did not know. It had happened again. His beloved 'Volksie' had gone – grabbed from him at gun-point. This time, he decided that he would take his uncle's advice.

It had been seven months since he had last spoken to his 'Eldorado' uncle. The fact that Uncle Boetie had not even bothered to attend the funeral of his own brother, Bafana, in Mapetla, Soweto, had made him bitter towards him. If Eldorado made one insensitive towards his own people then it was not worth living there. Perhaps Mavis was right after all. That was before the whole 'ibadi' (bad luck) happened again.

But now it had happened. His nice little 'Volksie' had gone, taken from him by an unscrupulous mob of youngsters in broad daylight. Where did they get the guns from anyway? He had been chatting away at Suzzie's Haunt and some time late in the afternoon, he decided to go to S'godiphola. In the bare veld over-looking the township, he saw the youths who came into

---

*   These are the different clauses which stipulate the legal
    required conditions under which a black person
    (African) may or may not qualify to stay or remain or
    work in the urban or so-called 'white' areas.

the road blocking him from passing. Something within him told him to run straight into them, but his dazed mind would not think straight. He slowed down when something inside him snapped with anger. He thought that if they attacked him outside, then he had a good chance of confusing them. It was only after he had slowed down that he realised that they were armed.

It was the next day. Velani could think clearly. He asked Mavis to go to work and leave him to his thoughts. If he were left alone, he would be able to figure out just how it happened.

He sat alone, his mind putting the pieces together.

After the no-good hoodlums had knocked him unconscious, they sped off in his 'Volksie' leaving him lying there. Some 'good Samaritan' – also a regular customer at Suzzie's Haunt – recognised him and picked him up. With some of their 'friends', they decided to take Velani first to the police station to report the loss of his car. When he, Velani, had regained consciousness, he had pleaded with his friends that he would rather go and report the matter to the police than go home 'on foot' to face his wife Mavis. They immediately rushed him to the nearby Moroka Police Station.

Never in his life had Velani seen so many people lined up in a small room waiting to be served. All of them had lost their cars. They all had sad stories to tell. Even sobbing women were there. Some of them had also been raped. It is only when you have your personal share of pain that you know what it is like to be pierced. Velani listened. His sense of loss had made him sober. He wondered how it was still possible for some of these people to speak about the pain at all, with their hearts still 'bleeding'. He listened, absent-minded. The two men next to him, with 'home-made' bandages tied around injured limbs, one an elbow and another his shin, rattled on in whispers, 'A friend of mine had his car interfered with and pushed-away right out of his yard, mind you; and he could do nothing! They were armed, so what could he do?'

The other confirmed, nodding all the time, 'I *know*. Others are hijacked at intersections. And when you come to report here they tell you that there are no policemen to come to your aid, that they are short of them. I'm not surprised. How can they be everywhere? Zambia, Malawi, Zimbabwe, Botswana, the Bantustans, Swaziland, Lesotho, the borders – all over. . . . What are they – an octopus?'

'It is dangerous these days to stop at a robot. Even when it is red, just dash on!'

Some sat looking hopefully at the official on the other side of the desk. The bespectacled policeman looked up at the rows of anxious, exhausted faces while he kept reaching for dockets. He seemed polite and Velani wondered what had happened. . . . He was thinking. . . . A so-called 'kaffer-konstabel' polite? Never. . . . Or was it in keeping with the so-called 'reform' process?. . . . So this was what they meant by 'reform', eh? It was a rather annoying revelation; especially because he kept on reiterating to one complainant after another, 'We can only try to do our best, but we cannot make promises that you'll get your cars. Soweto is bad. Most of you I know have no insurance cover. Too many cars are stolen. The thieves work fast. They use false number plates and they spray the cars almost immediately. It is difficult to spot any stolen car from the descriptions you give. . . . We are your friends. We are here to protect your property and your lives.'

The whole rhetoric sounded meaningless and hollow.

The sad people's eyes and ears were open, but they remained stern and unimpressed. Velani knew that he would never see his car again. It was gone for good. He could feel it in his blood.

Velani knew what he would do. He would ring his 'Eldorado' uncle and ask for advice. Perhaps he was right after all. What was the use of staying in Soweto? Who cares what happens to people in Soweto anyway? Certainly not the police or the so-called councillors or the law-makers in Pretoria.

As he sat alone, thinking, he became more and more certain that Boetie McCabel was in fact his best advisor. He only had had the common sense to look into the problem facing the blacks – especially the Africans – and arriving at the best solution to it. Escape . . . escape from the 'jungle' and draw closer to the well-provided-for world, the privileged one.

He reached for the telephone receiver and dialled the number impatiently, his brow sweating with excitement. It was the voice of a woman – possibly Mrs McCabel – which answered, 'Hello, kan ek u help?'

Velani replied, 'It's Mkhabela here, Ma'am. Can I speak to Mr McCabel please?'

'Just hold on please, I'll call him . . . Boetie!' she yelled, placing the receiver on the table. McCabel rushed from the kitchen into the lounge.

Velie recognised his uncle's voice immediately. He whispered into the receiver, 'Hello, it's Velie, Uncle Boetie. I want to come to Eldorado. I have decided to take your advice.'

'Why now?'

'My "Volksie" is gone. They took it again. Nothing is safe here. I want to come and live in Eldorado if . . .'

Before Velie could continue, McCabel interrupted,

'It's no use, Velie. The "disease" has spread all over. We also have "comrades" here. They want solidarity with the people of Soweto. They say they are returning to their roots. They have wiped off the numbers from the houses. They say unless we are one the struggle against the settlers is forever lost.

'Stay where you are. "Injury to one oppressed is injury to all," they say. We all have to change. Just like the police say, they cannot keep up with all the cases. Gangs of hooligans, encouraged and armed by the police themselves, are on the rampage and nobody really cares. All the police and army are really concerned about is tracking down the so-called "terrorists". It comes from the police themselves. They say they are tired, over-worked. People are no longer joining the police force. The few who are still there also want to go on strike. They want to run away and they don't know how to do it. . . . Are you still there Velie?'

Without another word, Velie dropped the receiver and sank on to the sofa next to him. He sighed and whispered to himself, 'It's no use. Real protection will come from the people themselves. From now on, I'm with the people.'

Gone are Those Days

This story was related to me by Aunt Lizzy, a former shebeen queen now living with her daughter and grand-children in Moroka Township, Soweto.

I have read the story about Newclare and I liked it because it reminded me of the days when I was still myself. We used to call Newclare 'Sdikidiki' then. There, life was really life. The streets were always full of people, young and old. Beggars, robbers, pickpockets, drunkards, prostitutes, prayer women, ministers – everything. But everybody was happy. I used to run a shebeen. They used to call me 'Chobolo', because I was really cheeky. I was 'hot'.

But you *are* still 'hot' Aunt Liz, I said, and she chuckled, smiling. She seemed to enjoy the reputation she had.

But in those days I was worse. With drinking people you have to be really strict, you know. If you are not, they can be very silly, you know. They try all sorts of tricks on you in order to evade paying. You let them drink first and pay later, that's no good. I had to learn that they must always 'babhadale k'qala, no nonsense'.

Why? I asked.

When they have finished drinking they start telling you that they have paid already and all that, they even become violent and threaten you. Some start making love to you, patting you on your backside and smiling so that you may forget that they have not paid you. Then I realised that they would take advantage of me because I was a widow, you see. They knew that I did not have a husband. I spoke to a half-brother of mine who was a boxer to come and help me. He used to knock everybody out in the boxing ring during his best days. He is a heavyweight and he had become even bigger then because he used to drink so much and was no longer boxing – in the boxing ring, I mean. But in the streets, he used to take no nonsense from anyone. So that's why I thought of using *him*. I asked him to come and help me but at the same time, I did not want him to scare my regular customers away, you know. His appearance alone would scare anybody. He was tall and hefty, very big.

Ao! I exclaimed.

Yes, he was a real giant of a man. But when I had given him a 'skaal'*, which was his 'pay' for the day, he would become very jolly and he liked to crack jokes. So as time went by my customers got used to him and they listened to his stories. He also liked them because they used to *share* their drinks with him. So we went on nicely together and I made a lot of money. We were like a big family *choir*.

Choir?

Yes. We used to sing hymns. You know some of

* 'skaal' = beer ration

94

these drunkards are very good at music – they *sing*!
Some used to be teachers, mind you; others choirboys
in church, and so on.

Did you also have women customers? I asked.

Of course. Where there are men, there are women.
But I do not favour them much because all they want to
do is to get as much money out of the men as possible.

But don't they also buy?

They do. But some of them like nice clothes and they
take the money from the drunk men to buy clothes,
lipstick, wigs and so on. And I don't like it because
some of these men's wives know their husbands drink
at my shebeen and they come to me to complain that
all their husbands' pay remains at my place. Some of
their wives are very cheeky and they *swear*. You would
hear a woman swear standing across the street, accusing
me of taking their husbands away from them, and letting
the shebeen women suck them of their pay. But that's
why I was happy I had 'Tallboy' (my big half-brother).

Were these women also scared of him?

Yes. Even you would be afraid of him. He was big
and ugly. He was especially ugly because he had lost
his four front teeth in a street fight with gangsters. They
attacked him. He was on his own and they were more
than ten.

Oh that was terrible! It was lucky that he did not die.

Yes. So it went so well in my shebeen that I used to
make a lot of money. But then, something happened
that spoilt everything. Everybody was no longer
drinking happily.

Why?

They started disturbing our peace and spoiling
everything.

Who? The customers?

No. The *police* with their Friday and Saturday night

raids. You know, we used to store our 'sgonfaan' outside in the yard. We dug big holes in the yard and buried large tin barrels in them. Then we brewed our beer and poured it in these buried barrels. Mine were many because I was busy. I had many customers. The police used to come on Friday night using crowbars, or long, sharp steel rods. They went into the yards and poked the ground all over detecting areas which sounded hollow. When they got to such a place, then you've *had* it. They would dig the container out and then destroy it. If they knew that it belonged to you, they would throw you into gaol for many months. It was terrible. They used to search every room in the yard. My room was in the corner, at the far end of the yard. We used to get a small boy and an old drunkard to stand at the gate and watch out for the police. Dogs barking also told us that the police had arrived. When the 'guards' saw them come, they would give a signal by whistling. All those drinking in the shebeen would run out and leave the 'scales' (old tin containers used for measuring). They used to give us a lot of trouble and so we thought of a good plan. We got empty tomato boxes and out of them Tallboy made a frame shaped exactly like a coffin, and patched it with pieces of cardboard. Then we covered it nicely with a black cloth and it looked just like a coffin. It had a nice lid on top and we kept some of the beer there. So when it was 'clear' some people sat on it and they drank happily and we used to sing. But when we heard the signal from the 'guards' outside, we just start singing a sad hymn loudly, and you know, Tallboy was very clever. He also made a black bib with a white collar and he went and borrowed a hymn book and a Bible. When the police hear the hymn, they just peep at the door and then they only find a 'priest' (Tallboy himself) standing and preaching or praying

while the 'mourners' kneel down round the 'coffin', and
we are having a 'mlindalo'. They they just go away
without disturbing us.

Aunt Liz was sitting there looking haggard and worried.
Yet she was trying to console me, speaking about the
good old days of Sophiatown. We were arrested in
Kanana; sitting in the wide yard with all the 'awaiting
trial' people. We had committed no offence. All we
wanted to do was to be left alone to bury my late uncle
in peace, and yet . . . I shook my head hopelessly. I
broke the silence because Aunt Liz would perhaps think
I was not listening.

But all this is like a dream now. We both nodded.

It's like a dream because if it were not, we would not
be sitting here, in Kanana, arrested for trespassing. How
can we be trespassing when we have only come to bury
my uncle? It's crazy, crazy, I tell you. To think that
Kanana means Canaan – 'the land of milk and honey'.
Yet we have come here, to this Boer town of
Klerksdorp, to be arrested.

And what on earth could have happened to Vusi?
Aunt Liz asked. We shook our heads.

The last time I saw him he was being pushed into the
'Kwela-Kwela'. He was pleading with them to let him
go and they would not let him go. They were certain
he was not one of the mourners. They accused him of
having hidden the guns. . . . 'Waar's die geweer; waar
het jy dit weggesteek? Komaan, praat!' (Where's the
gun; where did you hide it? Speak!)

And to think that that child never even touched a gun
in his life.

They must have taken him to some gaol somewhere.
Shall we ever see him again, I wonder. We shook our
heads again. I broke the silence.

I bet all this is because when they asked us we said we were from Soweto. When they saw the procession of cars coming in, they must have raised an alarm and panicked. We should not have disclosed that we were from Soweto. When the Boers hear the word Soweto, they see red, I tell you.

What's the use, we can't lie, can we?

What have we done wrong, anyway? And why has poor Vusi been taken? Where did they take him to? What happened to all the others? Uncle Bajama's widow – everybody – where are they? We are the only ones who were with the corpse.

They have many such barracks – sections and sections. The gaols are the only buildings they put up besides the beer halls. Even churches they fear these days. These days they don't leave us alone, never. Those days are dead and buried. Even when you are a corpse they don't leave you alone. My heart bleeds when I think of my dear brother. His corpse turned inside out like that!

What happened anyway? To me it was like a dream, a nightmare. The whole thing did not look real . . . the whole thing. Just then, I had been dreaming. It's strange how it happened. During the interval, after we had served the people with tea and cakes, I went into the bedroom to doze off a bit . . . just looked for a quite corner and squeezed myself in. In my dream, I was right back in Soweto again. You know the party for the sell-out called Thebe – the bloody 'S'banda' (headman) who should have been dead long long ago. . . . And now we were supposed to support the whole party business – the reception to welcome the new Township Manager, that dog, Vosloo. We had been told that the old one, Bezuidenhout, would open the whole ceremony. The 'leckies', the black policemen, they came round very early in the morning and woke us up. They said that all shebeen-owners should close on that day; that we have to come over and help with the cooking and serving of the 'big' guests – the white ones from town. It was very annoying, you know. We must leave our work for *that.* Then they turn back and tell us that we fail to pay all the 'heavy' rents they want from us. What are we, loafers? We are not loafers, we are trying to make a living for our families, our children. What do we care for Vosloo anyway? Where are we going to with him? Why couldn't they leave us alone, anyway? In my dream I had just thought of the plan.

What plan? Aunt Liz asked, puzzled.

The plan to get rid of these people once and for all. We came together like the true witches do. We made a conference. Each one of us had a suggestion. 'OK,' I suggested, 'we would get there and turn the whole thing into hell for the Vosloos, the Bezuidenhouts and all their leckies. We were going to exterminate them. Don't ask me how I knew the plan had worked because I knew all the same. In a dream you know everything. You see right into the hearts of people and you can tell what their feelings are. You can even feel what they feel, smell what they smell, even know what their pasts were like and see into their future. Once I was like the almighty God, with powers that surpass all understanding.

You could foresee what would happen like Nonquase, you mean; like a sangoma?

Yes, Aunt Liz, and even more. I was really powerful. All that I always wanted and wished to happen was going to happen. Everyone was going to respect my word. As we marched in, with me right at the head, leading the procession of shebeen queens, the white wasters and their wives were seated at either side of the two rows of tables laid with all sorts of food and refreshments. But as we filed in solemnly, each one of us had our hands tucked inside our aprons. We were all ready with different kinds of detergents and poisonous disinfectants. . . . Doom, Target, Surf, Persil, Punch, Rattex, Fumitabs, all of them. The guests were engrossed with themselves, their wives giggling and fanning their faces with fans in the bright sunshine. All of us, the cooks, took turns to empty the poisons into the big pots which were ready – full of gravies and soups. It was a well-planned conspiracy.

One by one, the guests fainted and turned their pink faces towards the sky. The members of the brass band must have joined in the conspiracy because they started playing a sad hymn, as if to bid them farewell on their journey to hell. They did not seem to mind when we poured the poisons into the gravy and soup pots.

It was while I was happily treading over their dead bodies that I woke up. But what was in front of me?

Was it when the policemen came in?

Yes. . . . I could not believe my eyes! Imagine a whole Boer boy. Who, in his or her wildest dreams, could ever think that right there, in that small match-box bedroom of my uncle's – dark and full of black mourners, one would see a white boy in police uniform wielding a torch and kicking everyone out of his way like that. These people must be dead scared – the cowards.

Two of them entered right into the bedroom with the coffin. Did you see them?

Yes. I was still dazed. I could not believe what I was seeing. If someone had told me the story I would never have believed it. I tell you they're now quite crazy. 'Open the box. Maak die kas oop!' he kept screaming. When no one obeyed he pushed the two wreaths with the gun and unscrewed the top off himself. What I saw when I woke up was an unbelievable sight . . . the pink face of a white boy in a police cap, his eyes peering into my uncle's coffin!

Not only peering. Didn't you see him turning the body over and poking, searching below it? What disgusts me is that they no longer even respect our customs. What did they hope to find there?

AK 47's – guns; hidden there under the corpse; brought in to exterminate them. They thought the whole funeral procession was a big lie. What do they care about our customs, about our dead? As long as they sit on us and they eat and drink, they don't care. Why do you think they left their own countries and went roaming around the whole world?

What is sickening is that when they had searched all over and found no guns, they did not even say 'sorry we made a mistake'.

To whom? How can they say 'sorry' to us?

And now, to crown it all, they arrested everybody from Soweto for trespass.

Leave them. One day we shall do the same thing to them; you wait and see.

'Elizabeth! Doris Mashinini . . . Stand up! Why did you not have permits to enter Kanaan Lokasi?'

We stood up and obeyed, taking our place in the long queue of 'trespass' prisoners.

Devil at a Dead End *

She arrived at Ficksburg Station at 2.30 p.m. It would be a good half-hour before the Durban train to Bethlehem arrived. The thought made her smile. She was early. Her mother would have congratulated her for the achievement. She remembered, with the smile still on her face, how she would always say to them, 'My children, learn to be in time always. The passenger should wait for the train, and not expect the train to wait for her.'

She descended the stairs facing the open window of the booking office. Through the round opening at eye-level, she could hear that the booking clerk was engaged in conversation with someone, a female.

She carefully placed a R10 banknote on the small, concave, coinerroded wooden base, letting it protrude into the other side through the semi-circular opening

---

* This story was banned in South Africa in 1979 before publication. The censorship board claimed at the time that because the story had been seen by two people (the postman and himself) it was as good as having been published.

over the plank. She waited, wondering about the contact and remembering what the taxi driver had said: 'You don't know this Boer clerk here. He can be very furious when you ask for a second-class ticket without having made a booking beforehand. Anyway, try. Speak to him in 'Se-Buru' and not English. They are more tolerant when you address them in their own language.'

'Ja?' the clerk said, banging impatiently on the base and startling her.

'Can I. . . . Kan ek 'n tweede-klas kaartjie kry na Johannesburg-toe, asseblief?'

'Het jy bespreking gemaak?'

'Nee, ek . . .'

'Wel, nee. Natuurlik kan jy nie!' he snapped.

And without much ado, he grabbed the money and deposited (or shall I say he flung) a ticket and change in banknotes with some silver and bronze coins on the base. The girl tried to plead, saying she was from very far away, in the outlying areas of Leribe district in Lesotho. The clerk gazed at her, his fierce-looking, cat-like, bespectacled grey eyes looking like an abyss, with the pupils dilating and contracting. She flinched and dropped her eyes. In that instant, the furious clerk grunted with a hard bang, drew the wooden shutter over the window-pane. The girl bent down slowly. A black railway policeman who was standing a few metres away scurried nearer, and together, they picked up some of the coins which had landed on the concrete floor. He asked, 'Did you want a second-class ticket, my sister?'

'Yes.'

'They usually insist that you make a booking two weeks before the intended date of departure.'

'How does one make a booking when you come from

so far away? I would have to spend two days along the way. You know where Nqechane is.'

'I know,' said the policeman, nodding. 'And when you make a booking by phone, they ignore you. Some even try sending telegrams; but these are never noted. Anyway, don't worry. When you get to Bethlehem, ask the ticket examiner to convert your ticket to second class. The new Line trains via Balfour are usually never fully booked. Then at least you won't have to stand the whole night right up to Johannesburg.'

The siren of the oncoming steam locomotive became audible and minutes later the train pulled into the platform. The kind policeman helped the girl into the packed third-class coach and one of the passengers on the train extended his arms to receive the girl's bags. She thanked both men for their courtesy.

There seemed to be no sitting space available, and there was no point in attempting to move any further than where she was. She leaned against a window and arranged her three bags on the floor along the side of the passage wall. One bag she clamped between her feet and the other two she nestled against her jutting slim ankles. She could at least *feel* her bags all the time, she thought gratefully, as she clung to her handbag.

The train moved on slowly, stopping at the many sidings and stations and winding its way laboriously over the steep slopes. She closed her eyes and listened, wishing that she were at least lying down. That distance she had walked on foot! She thought of the booking clerk at Ficksburg and his eyes.

'It will be raining by the time we get to Bethlehem, can you see that, my sister?'

Only then was she aware of the presence of the kind man who had received her on to the train. She opened her eyes and noticed that the clouds were gathering fast and she nodded in response to the question. She could not make out whether the young man was coloured or Indian or African; she finally decided to dismiss the matter and not let her mind dwell on it. She looked through the open window into the peaceful receding landscape outside. Her searching eyes quickly spotted the mountain peak of Nqechane and she thought of the tranquillity of the past three weeks she had spent at the beautiful village bearing the name of the peak. Everything was just as she remembered it when she was still a child.

She closed her eyes and her thoughts drifted on, rocked by the swaying rhythmic movements of the train. . . . She thought of the horrible eyes of the booking clerk at Ficksburg.

She recollected that she had not been in contact with a single white person for the duration of her holiday. She had had perfect peace. No; she corrected herself – with the exception of 'Mè Sistèrè', the Mother Superior at the nearby Nqechane Anglican Mission, and 'Ntate Fatèrè', the Priest-in-Charge. But those were different, she argued with herself. They even extended a friendly arm to greet you. That is why she had forgotten about them. But of course there was her first contact with those white people at the border post of Ficksburg* – how on earth could she forget that? She could not remember that contact because she had the Open-Sesame – the *brown* Travel Document of the Republic and not the *green* Lesotho Local Passport. It was precisely because of those first *contacts* that she had at last decided to change from green to brown. The

---

* Border between Lesotho and South Africa. Crossing into South Africa is always confrontational and often traumatic for Blacks.

nauseating numerous questions they used to ask when you wanted to come to any part of this Republic, especially Johannesburg. As if crossing a mere river meant the same thing as going from heaven to hell or vice versa. What did it matter what you crossed to get where anyway? They would ask you:

Why do you want to go to Johannesburg?
To what address?
How long are you going to be there?
Who is the person you are visiting there?
How much money have you got in your purse – will you be able to pay for a return ticket?

And more often than not, you would be refused permission. Your *green* document would be flung at you and you would have to turn right back with your carefully prepared chicken provision and dumplings in your tin trunk and all. They wouldn't even consider the sacrifices you made to get to that post at all. Like how many days and nights you travelled on foot; or whether there are any buses where you come from; or if there are buses, whether you were able to pay the fare or not. Whether your reasons for visiting the Republic were valid or not depended mainly on whether the 'nonnie' had prepared a good breakfast for the particular 'baas' at the post at the time or not. Of late, even when you claimed that there was a death of a close relation of yours at that address in the Republic they would turn you back. *Death*, not illness, Death – what is worse than Death? And even if you actually produced a telegram to prove your claim they were not ashamed to ask you whether you were going to *eat* that corpse. 'What are you going to do with the dead person?' they ask you. She remembered how when she got tired of all those stinking questions, she had taken the advice of her friend: leave the green thing in the bag and cross the river – walk or swim over it or across it, that's all.

But that too presented problems: the inevitable arrangements with the 'professional' river escorts, the ones who knew, or professed to know, when, where, and how to cross the Caledon in order to avoid contact with the whites at the border post with your green book. Armed sentries are known to carry on continuous patrols along the banks of the river. And these do not hesitate to open fire. These are some of the reasons which make those escorts indispensable. In addition, the escorts would have to come to some agreement with the inspectors at the customs barriers. These would have to pass your luggage without asking too many questions. Some prior negotiations with people near the river on the other side to accommodate you where you could sit and dry your clothes while you waited to be reunited with your luggage. Some accidents were known to happen and this could incur heavy losses of valuables especially if the escorts were not adequately compensated. The whole process became more and more expensive.

She thought of the last straw, when she decided to bury her green book for ever and vowed to go to any lengths to acquire a brown one. She recalled bitterly that it was all because of that abominable barbed wire fence. Who ever thought that those white officials on this side would ever think of going to the extent of actually erecting a barbed wire fence right along the meandering Caledon River? Honestly! Just to bring about that contact. She had first to be carried across the full river, and then over a nearly seven-foot-high barbed wire fence by yelling, giggling, curious youths who obviously found it amusing and gratifying – the experience of coddling ordinarily inaccessible parts of the anatomy of a partially clad woman! She had her *brown* travel documents in her handbag now, and all that ordeal was over, thank God.

She thought of those eyes of the white booking clerk.

Just after 6 p.m., the train steamed steadily into Platform One at Bethlehem. A strong wind blew from the Drakensberg Mountains in the east and swept the raindrops into the faces of the alighting passengers, now rushing towards the smelly non-white waiting-rooms just outside the station, about twenty metres from the railway line.

'I will take these, my sister,' said the voice of the kind young man, relieving her of two of her bags.

'Thanks,' she said.

They joined the seemingly endless moving stream of passengers to the waiting-rooms.

At exactly 7 p.m. the black announcer came round swinging a large loudspeaker and shouting into its mouthpiece, 'Ba eang Gauteng ba ee ho Platform Three! Ba eang Gauteng ba ee ho Platform Three! . . .'

Still accompanied by the willing strange young man, the girl followed the long procession over the narrow bridge.

On Platform Three, there were two guards standing and chatting near the wooden benches. The girl said to the young man, 'I want to ask the guard to convert my ticket from third-to second-class, but I'm reluctant. I travelled on foot and by bus the whole day and I'm tired. I wouldn't be able to stand the whole night right to Johannesburg.'

'Where are you from, my sister?'

'Nqechane, in the Leribe District.'

'Oh. I don't even know where that is; I'm from Bloemfontein. Do go. I'll accompany you into the compartment and return to the third-class coaches.'

'And where are *you* going to?'

'Also Johannesburg.'

Reluctantly, and with a feeling of apprehension, the girl moved towards the two guards, who looked at her questioningly as she approached. She suddenly became conscious of her high platform shoes. She moved slowly. She would have to avoid the risk of tripping, she thought. She was thankful that her wide-bottomed balooba denim pair of slacks concealed her knees which were by now impulsively knocking against each other. Her step, which was normally graceful and confident, was faltering. . . . She thought of the white booking clerk at Ficksburg. Not knowing who of the two white men to refer her request to, she held her ticket before them and asked, 'Kan ek hierdie kaartjie verander tot tweede-klas asseblief?'

And without appearing to pay much attention, the man on her right-hand side said, signalling to the nearby coach with the 'Non-Whites – Reserved' sign on it, 'Gaan in die "C" Kompartement.'

With great relief and a smile on her face, she obeyed. She had been fortunate . . . She thought of the furious eyes of the clerk at the booking office in Ficksburg. On her way, she passed the 'B' compartment and noticed that there was only one black lady in it. She smiled and nodded expectantly when the girl greeted her. The girl hesitated. She stopped and asked her, 'Are you with other passengers in here, Mother?'

'No, my child, I'm alone in here. Haven't seen any others arriving.'

He *did* say 'C', she thought, puzzled.

She passed on to the next compartment. It was also unoccupied. She put her bags on the cushioned green bunk. She looked around. It was clean and comfortable – a welcome change from the third-class coaches she had been standing in from Ficksburg. Only the stale familiar odour of the inevitable Dettol that, she had come to know, one would have to learn to live with. It was permanent, and it seemed to have been built into the very heavily wood-panelled walls of the compartments. Like the inlaid, meaningless landscape photographs of the sunny South Africa which seemed to strive to create beauty in surroundings where most of the time only ugliness and cruelty prevailed.

She decided to speak to the elderly lady next-door. After exchanging the usual formalities, she remarked, 'I wonder why the guard said I must go into "C" when you are alone here. The usual procedure is to let females share the same compartment, and the male passengers also their own, isn't it?'

'I wondered why you passed into "C", but then I thought you had more ladies accompanying you, my child.'

'No. I'm alone.'

They both smiled. She folded her arms over her bosom and sighed, still smiling, and remarked, twisting the ends of her lips and raising her eyebrows, 'Perhaps he wants to pay you a visit.'

'A visit?' the girl asked, surprised. . . . She thought of the booking clerk at Ficksburg, and realised that she would have the image of those grey cruel eyes on her for a long time. She said, 'I don't think he'd do that.'

'Why, my child?'

The girl shrugged her shoulders vigorously, and answered, 'I don't know. But somehow they don't seem to know that we are human beings like *them*.'

'You're still very young, aren't you?' and she peeped through the window, pointing. 'You see that train in that platform on the other side? It's full of soldiers. All those white soldiers there, can you see them?'

'Yes. All carrying guns and filing into the train with kitbags. What about them?'

'Yes. They're soldiers. I don't know who they are fighting or why. One teacher told me that they are fighting black people somewhere in the north. They have a big camp just outside Bethlehem. That's where they learn how to shoot and all about fighting. When you pass there, you'll always see them drilling, playing all sorts of games. No black woman moves in that area without men to protect her. They chase them into the dongas and grab them by force. Would they do that if they didn't think we're humans?'

The girl shook her head. 'I'd like to go into the cloakroom or toilet there and do some washing up before I sit and eat something. Shall I leave my bags in your compartment? Surely he can't expect me to sit alone there. What happens if I should want to visit the small house, take everything with me? The same thing applies with *you* too. People want to sit together and speak. It can be very lonely. I'd rather be in here with you.'

The train left Bethlehem. The ticket examiner came and issued the new second-class ticket without appearing to notice anything amiss or out of order. He did not seem to mind the two women being together. They both ordered bedding. He was very formal and to the point; he then left.

'I'll wait until you come back, then it will be my turn and you can stay with the luggage.'

The girl left, taking her handbag and adding into it a few of the items she would need. She returned about twelve minutes later, feeling refreshed and no longer so tired. 'It's *your* turn now, Mother,' she said to the smiling lady.

'Hm. . . . You smell sweet, and look like a fresh peach!'

'Thanks.' The girl blushed.

She was just reaching up to ease her sling bag into the baggage rack above, when the guard stood at the door. He looked at the girl noticing the bare portion of her ebony torso and the pronounced umbilical groove, reducing her slim waistline even more. Trying to look at him and noticing his fixed stare, she withdrew her arm almost instinctively and readjusted the hem of her short blouse. She pulled it down to cover her bare waist and felt uncomfortable when he shifted his eyes from her body to meet hers.

'Where's your companion?' he asked, smiling and frowning.

'Who?'

'Your escort or husband. The man who was with you when you entered the coach.'

'Oh. He. . . .'

The man did not wait to hear what the girl said because just then, the elderly woman appeared at the end of the narrow passage and he moved away, tapping at the next door, smiling and giving her way to pass. She went into the compartment and shut the door behind her, whispering and smiling. 'What did I tell you? Didn't I tell you that he'd pay you a visit?'

'He asked me where the man who was carrying my bags had gone to. He said something about "husband" and when I tried to explain, he saw *you* coming and just left.'

'Oh, jealous!'

They both laughed.

'He knows I'm getting off at Villiers; but don't worry, it will be dawn already. I suppose he'll get tired of waiting.'

Not long after they had shared their provisions, and they had exhausted their long 'introductions' in the usual African way, the coloured attendant came to prepare their beds from the 'non-white' bedding kits. They went to bed and switched off the lights. The swaying train and the steady drizzle outside lulled them into a peaceful sleep as it traversed the unending beautiful maize fields.

During the early hours of the morning, the guard knocked at the door to warn the elderly lady that the train was nearing Villiers, and disappeared. She felt reluctant to wake up the girl to bid her goodbye; thinking that she might find it difficult to sleep again after her departure. She decided to wake her up, anyway, as she felt just that it would be cruel for her to walk out. She bade the girl farewell and assured her that there was the coloured attendant in the nearby compartment and that she thought she had heard other passengers move into the other compartments. She explained, 'I know most third-class people usually come to the coach where the guard is only to get their tickets and then go back to third. But perhaps some of them were second-class passengers.' She bent down and whispered into the girl's ear, 'I don't think he'll ignore their presence. Besides – the law! Just make sure you lock the door from inside, my child.'

The train glided out of the platform. It was a smooth quiet motion and she remembered that the coaches were now being drawn by an electric engine. She lay quietly, listening. . . . She thought of the ticket examiner's strange behaviour, and she remembered those eyes of the booking clerk at Ficksburg station.

From afar, came the low rumble of thunder. She moved out of her bed and walked to the other window, rolled up the blind and opened it. She looked out. The wide expanse of farm-lands lay completely deserted, enveloped in pitch-black darkness. The lights piercing through the train windows struck the falling raindrops and formed rays of oblique streaks of glittering lines, descending heavily against the side of the coaches. The rain was pouring in torrents. There was no sign of life in the coach in which she was. Where was the coloured attendant anyway, fast asleep, she wondered. Was Johannesburg still far to go? She could not sleep.

The train stopped. It was a big station – 'Balfour North', the sign read. When the train was about to leave, the guard emerged from a room on the platform and stood next to the train facing expectantly towards the fore end. He noticed the girl withdraw her head into the compartment, and draw the blinds.

He blew his whistle and shouted, 'Balfour North!' and the train pulled out of the platform.

The door yielded easily when the guard prised the lever with his key. She turned, startled, and aware that she was scantily dressed in her flimsy nightie. She tried to move towards her bed and he intercepted her saying, 'It's dark. You needn't be afraid. I've just come to chat with you that's all, please. I'm lonely in my cubicle, please. Please,' he begged, speaking calmly.

She asked, 'Chat about what?'

He smiled, asking, 'Where did you say your husband went to?'

'He's not my husband. He was a stranger. He helped me carry my luggage over the steps in Bethlehem.'

'What is he of yours?'

'What do you mean?'

'Can I turn on the very dim light, please? I like to see your beautiful face; can I?' the man said, reaching for the switch. The dim light came on. He smiled into the girl's face, and she drew away.

'I mean; is he your "nyatsi" or what?' he said, twisting his eyebrows and smiling mischievously.

She sat on the cushioned bunk and watched him remove his cap and put it on the steel peg above the door. It struck her that the man's manner and tone of speech, which had been formal and austere in the presence of the middle-aged lady, had now changed to familiarity. His behaviour had altered like a reversible cloak; like a garment you either decided to keep on or strip off, just like that. She was not sure she liked the metamorphosis, but she became more curious. . . . She thought of the Ficksburg station booking clerk's eyes.

She remembered that she once heard a person saying that most whites first learnt swear words in the vocabulary of the African languages. She asked, 'What did you say he was of mine?'

'Your "nyatsi"', he repeated, emphasising the word.

'We travelled together from Ficksburg. He helped me with my baggage; and I was late. The train nearly left me. I was lucky to meet a sympathetic person.'

'Why were you late? Flirting, I suppose.'

'No. I was pleading with the booking clerk to sell me a second-class ticket and he was refusing.'

'And so your companion came to *console* you?' and he mentioned the word 'troos' (console) already moving towards her. He asked, 'How about letting *me* do that, then? I'd like to comfort you. I'd enjoy it very much,' he said, coming near her as the girl receded, petrified. 'Don't be afraid, please. Come; just stand up. Come, man; don't be so lazy. Just stand up and let's have some fun. Just a little love making,' the guard implored, touching her slim shoulders tenderly and stroking them. 'Come. It won't hurt, please. Come on, hold me tight, tight!' he demanded, taking the girl's hands and crossing them behind him. The girl slackened her grip, but he stopped her. 'Don't do that, please. All right, just clasp me tightly against you and I'll be satisfied.'

He held her face in both his hands and pressed it against his warm, impetuous body, raising her chin. The girl closed her eyes. 'Don't close your eyes, please. They're *so* beautiful. Look at me. Look into my eyes, please.'

The girl kept her eyes closed. She was thinking of the haunting, furious eyes of the booking clerk at Ficksburg. He switched off the light. 'Come now. Stand up. We shall soon be in Johannesburg. Please. You're hard, man – unyielding. Why?' he asked. He looked at his wrist watch in the dark. The green arms and the circle of dots were vivid and luminous. 'Just wait for me; I'm coming. There's a station nearby.'

The girl sat trembling and feeling guilty. She reprimanded herself, I should be screaming for help or something. She sat waiting. She was surprised at herself. She had been like a bewildered beholder, powerless. She had abandoned herself into the arms of a strange white man who did not even know her name. An expert who obviously knew what he was doing. She was taken aback at what seemed to be a response by a part of herself over which she had no control. She felt like a being apart, looking on. She waited, dismayed.

She listened. It was quiet outside. The storm had subsided. There was no downpour here. The torrent seemed to have been cut with a knife.

She heard the now-familiar voice of the ticket examiner. He yelled, 'Union!'

The train glided slowly out of the platform.

The next moment, the guard darted stealthily up the two steps in a single stride. He sneaked quietly into the dimly lit compartment. Without uttering a word, and with one powerful wrench, he gathered the tender body of the woman in his arms and her face came to rest against his. He breathed the words tenderly into her ear, 'Come on now, please!'

She slowly wrapped her shaky reluctant arms around the warm neck of the guard. They stood there and kissed. She could feel his strong muscles move as he gently stroked her back. He moved his exploring hands down her midriff and below. His knees seemed to sag and he knelt on the edge of the cushioned bunk. As his left hand caressed the girl's firm nipple, his right hand felt for the switch and lowered it. The darkness surrounded them completely, isolating them from the rest of the world. She thought of the fiery, bottomless eyes of the booking clerk at Ficksburg station.

Almost in a whisper, his warm breath pouring like steam over her naked body, he pleaded. 'Kom,' he said, 'kom nou, toe, kom. Dis net die twee van ons; toemaar. Dis net ons twee; kom.'

In the darkness, and with his eyes closed tightly, his warm quavering, salivating tongue groped towards the girl's navel, and spotting it, sank into its hollow warmness.

'Oh God help me. Let *something* happen. . . .' The girl's conscience, her soul, stood aloof, untouched, admonishing. Her heart was pounding fast, but only with a feeling of guilt. 'What if my parents, my husband. . . . What if . . . ? Oh no, no, no!'

Still kneeling and salivating like Pavlov's dog, the man continued to plead anxiously, 'Kom nou, kom . . . ag tog . . . asseblief, kom . . .'

She drew a deep breath, lifting her face and looking up into the darkness; waiting for something, some miracle.

In times of threat, some invisible omnipotent power seems always to be waiting to come to the aid of the helpless, the weak, the defenceless. It was not through a cannon that David vanquished Goliath.

The girl remembered. . . . Somewhere in the Christian scriptures, they say, a maiden had hidden a potion in her bosom, and she did not want to be searched. The words entered her mind and she uttered them mechanically: 'Ntate se nkame hobane ke silafetse. . . .' Her lips mumbled the entreaty, softly and uncertainly. . . . 'Father, do not touch me because I am unclean. . . .'

Then repeating loudly, drawing back and pushing the kneeling man, she gasped, 'Se nkame hobane ke silafetse . . . ke metse *mokoala*!' (Do not touch me because I am afflicted with a venereal sickness.)

'Mokaola!' . . . One of those detestable, ominous words. The impact of that word was quick, merciless, shocking and immediately disarming. Like when in a dark alley you suddenly grope into a dead end. She stood still listening to the sound of receding breath. She reached below the bunk above and lowered the dim switch. She watched the recoiling devilish figure and drew a sigh of relief.

The Point of No Return

S'bongile stopped at the corner of Sauer and Jeppe Streets and looked up at the robot. As she waited for the green light to go on, she realised from the throbbing of her heart and her quick breathing that she had been moving too fast. For the first time since she had left Senaoane, she became conscious of the weight of Gugu, strapped tightly on her back.

All the way from home, travelling first by bus and then by train from Nhlanzane to Westgate Station, her thoughts had dwelt on Mojalefa, the father of her baby. Despite all efforts to forget, her mind had continually reverted to the awesome results of what might lie ahead for them, if they (Mojalefa and the other men) carried out their plans to challenge the government of the Republic of South Africa.

The incessant rumbling of traffic on the two intersecting one-way streets partially muffled the eager male voices audible through the open windows on the second floor of Myler House on the other side of the street. The men were singing freedom songs. She stood and listened for a while before she crossed the street.

Although he showed no sign of emotion, it came as

a surprise to Mojalefa when one of the men told him that a lady was downstairs waiting to see him. He guessed that it must be S'bongile and he felt elated at the prospect of seeing her. He quickly descended the two flights of stairs to the foyer. His heart missed a beat when he saw her.

'*Ao banna!*' he said softly as he stood next to her, unable to conceal his feelings. He looked down at her and the baby, sleeping soundly on her back. S'bongile slowly turned her head to look at him, taken aback at his exclamation. He bent down slightly and brushed his dry lips lightly over her forehead just below her neatly plaited hair. He murmured, 'It's good to see you again, Bongi. You are *so* beautiful! Come, let's sit over here.'

He led her away from the stairs, to a wooden bench further away opposite a narrow dusty window overlooking the courtyard. A dim ray of light pierced through the window-panes making that spot the only bright area in the dimly lit foyer.

He took out a piece of tissue from his coat-pocket, wiped off the dust from the sill and sat down facing her. He said, 'I'm very happy you came. I . . .'

'I *had* to come, Mojalefa,' she interrupted.

'I could not bear it any longer; I could not get my mind off the quarrel. I could not do any work, everything I picked up kept falling out of my hands. Even the washing I tried to do I could not get done. I *had* to leave everything and come. I kept thinking of you . . . as if it was all over, and I would not see you nor touch you ever again. I came to convince myself that I could still see you as a free man; that I could still come close to you and touch you. Mojalefa, I'm sorry I behaved like that last night. I thought you were indifferent to what I was going through. I was jealous because you kept on telling me that you were committed. That like all the others, you had already resigned from your job, and that there was no turning back. I thought you cared more for the course you have chosen than for Gugu and me.'

'There's no need for you to apologise, Bongi, I never blamed you for behaving like that and I bear you no malice at all. All I want from you is that you should understand. Can we not talk about something else? I am so happy you came.'

They sat looking at each other in silence. There was *so* much they wanted to say to one another, just this once. Yet both felt tongue-tied; they could not think of the right thing to say. She felt uneasy, just sitting there and looking at him while time was running out for them. She wanted to steer off the painful subject of their parting, so she said, 'I have not yet submitted those forms to Baragwanath. They want the applicants to send them in together with their pass numbers. You've always discouraged me from going for a pass, and now they want a number. It's almost certain they'll accept me because of my matric certificate. That is if I submit my form *with the number* by the end of this month, of course. What do you think I should do, go for registration? Many women and girls are already rushing to the registration centres. They say it's useless for us to refuse to carry them like you men because we will not be allowed to go anywhere for a visit or buy anything valuable. And now the hospitals, too . . .'

'No, no wait. . . . Wait until. . . . Until after this. . . . After you know what the outcome is of what we are about to do.'

Mojalefa shook his head. It was intolerable. Everything that happened around you just went to emphasise the hopelessness of even trying to live like a human being. Imagine a woman having to carry a pass everywhere she goes; being stopped and searched or ordered to produce her pass! This was outrageous, the ultimate desecration and an insult to her very existence. He had already seen some of these 'simple' women who come to seek work from 'outside', proudly moving in the streets with those plastic containers dangling round their necks like sling bags. He immediately thought of the tied-down bitch and it nauseated him.

S'bongile stopped talking. She had tried to change the topic from the matter of their parting but now she could discern that she had only succeeded in making his thoughts wander away into a world unknown to her. She felt as if he had shut her out, aloof. She needed his nearness, now more than ever. She attempted to draw him closer to herself; to be *with* him just this last time. She could not think of anything to say. She sat listening to the music coming from the upper floors. She remarked, 'That music, those two songs they have just been singing; I haven't heard them before. Who composes them?'

'Most of the men contribute something now and again. Some melodies are from old times, they just supply the appropriate words. Some learn "new" tunes from old people at home, old songs from our past. Some are very old. Some of our boys have attended the tribal dancing ceremonies on the mines and they learn these during the festivities. Most of these are spontaneous, they come from the feelings of the people as they go about their work; mostly labourers. Don't you sometimes hear them chanting to rhythm as they perform tasks; carrying heavy iron bars or timber blocks along the railway lines or road construction sites? They even sing about the white foreman who sits smoking a pipe and watches them as they sweat.'

S'bongile sat morose, looking towards the entrance at the multitudes moving towards the centre of town and down towards Newtown. She doubted whether any of those people knew anything of the plans of the men who were singing of the aspirations of the blacks and their hopes for the happier South Africa they were envisaging. Her face, although beautiful as ever, reflected her depressed state. She nodded in half-hearted approval at his enthusiastic efforts to explain. He went on, 'Most of the songs are in fact lamentations – they reflect the disposition of the people. We shall be thundering them tomorrow morning on our way as we march towards the gaols of this country!'

With her eyes still focussed on the stream of pedestrians and without stopping to think, she asked, 'Isn't it a bit premature? Going, I mean. You are *so* few; a drop in an ocean.'

'It isn't numbers that count, Bongi,' he answered, forcing a smile. How many times had he had to go through that, he asked himself. In the trains, the buses, at work . . . Bongi was unyielding. Her refusal to accept that he must go was animated by her selfish love, the fear of facing life without him. He tried to explain although he had long realised that his efforts would always be fruitless. It was also clear to him that it was futile to try and run away from the issue.

'In any case,' he went on, 'it will be up to *you*, the ones who remain behind, the women and the mothers, to motivate those who are still dragging their feet; you'll remain only to show them why they must follow in our footsteps. That the future and dignity of the blacks as a nation and as human beings is worth sacrificing for.'

Her reply only served to demonstrate to him that he might just as well have kept quiet. She remarked, 'Even your father feels that this is of no use. He thinks it

123

would perhaps only work if all of you first went out to *educate* the people so that they may join in.'

'No, father does not understand. He thinks we are too few as compared to the millions of all the black people of this land. He feels that we are sticking out our necks. That we can never hope to get the white man to sit round a table and speak to us, here. All he'll do is order his police to shoot us dead. If they don't do that, then they'll throw us into the gaols, and we shall either die there or be released with all sorts of afflictions. It's because I'm his only son. He's thinking of *himself*, Bongi, he does not understand.'

'He *does* understand, and he loves you.'

'Maybe that's *just* where the trouble lies. Because he loves me, he fails to think and reason properly. We do not agree. He is a different kind of person from me, and he can't accept that. He wants me to speak, act, and even think like him, and that is impossible.'

'He wants to be proud of you, Mojalefa.'

'If he can't be proud of me as I am, then he'll never be. He says I've changed. That I've turned against everything he taught me. He wants me to go to church regularly and pray more often. I sometimes feel he hates me, and I sympathise with him.'

'He does not hate you, Mojalefa; you two just do not see eye to eye.'

'My father moves around with a broken heart. He feels I am a renegade, a disappointment; an embarrassment to him. You see, as a preacher, he has to stand before the congregation every Sunday and preach on the importance of obedience, of how as Christians we have to be submissive and tolerant and respect those who are in authority over us under all conditions. That we should leave it to "the hand of God" to right all wrongs. As a reprisal against all injustices we must kneel down and pray because, as the scriptures tell us, God said, "Vengeance is Mine." He wants me to follow in his footsteps.'

'Be a priest or preacher, you mean?'

'Yes. Or show some interest in his part-time ministry. Sing in the church choir and so on, like when I was still a child.' He smiled wryly.

'Why don't you show *some* interest then? Even if it is only for his sake? Aren't you a Christian, don't you believe in God?'

'I suppose I do. But not like *him* and those like him, no.'

'What is *that* supposed to mean?'

'What's the use of praying all the time? In the first place, how can a slave kneel down and pray without feeling that he is not quite a man, human? Every time I try to pray I keep asking myself - if God loves me like the Bible says he does, then why should I have to carry a pass? Why should I have to be a virtual tramp in the land of my forefathers, why? Why should I have all these obnoxious laws passed against me?'

Then the baby on Bongi's back coughed, and Mojalefa's eyes drifted slowly towards it. He looked at the sleeping Gugu tenderly for a while and sighed, a sad expression passing over his eyes. He wanted to say something but hesitated and kept quiet.

Bongi felt the strap cutting painfully into her shoulder muscles and decided to transfer the baby to her lap. Mojalefa paced up and down in the small space, deep in thought. Bongi said, 'I have to breast-feed him. He hasn't had his last feed. I forgot everything. I just grabbed him and came here, and he didn't cry or complain. Sometimes I wish he would cry more often like other children.'

Mojalefa watched her suckling the baby. He reluctantly picked up the tiny clasped fist and eased his thumb slowly into it so as not to rouse the child. The chubby fingers immediately caressed his thumb and embraced it tightly. His heart sank, and there was a lump in his throat. He had a strong urge to relieve S'bongile of the child, pick him up in his strong arms and kiss him, but he suppressed the desire. It was at times like these that he experienced great conflict. He said, 'I should never have met you, Bongi. I am not worthy of your love.'

'It was cruel of you, Mojalefa. All along you knew you would have to go, and yet you made me fall for you. You made me feel that life without you is no life at all. Why did you do this to me?'

He unclasped his thumb slowly from the baby's instinctive clutch, stroking it tenderly for a moment. He walked slowly towards the dim dusty window. He looked through into the barely visible yard, over the roofs of the nearby buildings, into the clear blue sky above. He said, 'It is because I have the belief that we shall meet again, Bongi; that we shall meet again, in a free Africa!'

The music rose in a slow crescendo.

'That song. It is so *sad*. It sounds like a hymn.'

They were both silent. The thoughts of both of them anchored on how unbearable the other's absence would be. Mojalefa consoled himself that at least he knew his father would be able to provide the infant with all its needs. That he was fortunate and not like some of his colleagues who had been ready – in the midst of severe poverty – to sacrifice all. Thinking of some of them humbled him a great deal. S'bongile would perhaps be accepted in Baragwanath where she would take up training as a nurse. He very much wanted to break the silence. He went near his wife and touched her arm. He whispered, 'Promise me, Bongi, that you will do your best. That you will look after him, please.'

'I *shall*. He is our valuable keepsake – your father's and mine – something to remind me of you. A link nobody can destroy. All yours and mine.'

He left her and started pacing again. He searched hopelessly in his mind for something to say; something pleasant. He wanted to drown the sudden whirl of emotion he felt in his heart when he looked down at S'bongile, his young bride of only a few weeks, and the two-month-old child he had brought into this world.

S'bongile came to his rescue. She said, 'I did not tell my mother that I was coming here. I said that I was taking Gugu over to your father for a visit. He is always so happy to see him.'

Thankful for the change of topic, Mojalefa replied, smiling, 'You know, my father is a strange man. He is unpredictable. For instance, when I had put you into trouble and we realised to our horror that Gugu was on the way, I thought that he would skin me alive, that *that* was now the last straw. I did not know how I would approach him, because then it was clear that you would also have to explain to your mother why you would not be in a position to start at Turfloop. There was also the thought that your mother had paid all the fees for your first year and had bought you all those clothes and so forth. It nearly drove me mad worrying about the whole mess. I kept thinking of your poor widowed mother; how she had toiled and saved so that you would be able to start at university after having waited a whole year for the chance. I decided to go and tell my uncle in Pretoria and send *him* to face my father with the catastrophic announcement. I stayed away from home for weeks after that.'

'Oh yes, it was nerve-racking, wasn't it? And they

were all so kind to us. After the initial shock, I mean. We have to remember that all our lives, and be thankful for the kind of parents God gave us. I worried *so* much, I even contemplated suicide, you know. Oh well, I suppose you could not help yourself!'

She sighed deeply, shaking her head slowly. Mojalefa continued, 'Mind you, I knew something like that would happen, yet I went right ahead and talked you into yielding to me. I was drawn to you by a force so great, I just could not resist it. I hated myself for weeks after that. I actually despised myself. What is worse is that I had vowed to myself that I would never bring into this world a soul that would have to inherit my servitude. I had failed to "develop and show a true respect for our African womanhood", a clause we are very proud of in our disciplinary code, and I remonstrated with myself for my weakness.'

'But your father came personally to see my people and apologise for what you had done, and later to pay all the *lobola* they wanted. He said that we would have to marry immediately as against what you had said to me – why it would not be wise for us to marry, I mean.'

'That was when I had gone through worse nightmares. I had to explain to him why I did not want to tie you down to me when I felt that I would not be able to offer you anything, that I would only make you unhappy. You know why I was against us marrying, Bongi, of course. I wanted you to be free to marry a "better" man, and I had no doubt it would not be long before he grabbed you. Any man would be proud to have you as his wife, even with a child who is not his.'

He touched her smooth cheek with the back of his hand, and added, 'You possess those rare delicate attributes that any man would want to feel around him and be enkindled by.'

'Your father would never let Gugu go, not for anything, Mojalefa. He did not name him "his pride" for nothing. I should be thankful that I met the son of a person like that. Not all women are so fortunate. How many beautiful girls have been deserted by their lovers and are roaming the streets with illegitimate babies on their backs, children they cannot support?'

'I think it is an unforgivable sin. And not all those men do it intentionally, mind you. Sometimes, with all their good intentions, they just do not have the means to do much about the problem of having to pay *lobola*, so they disappear, and the girls never see them again.'

'How long do you think they'll lock you up, Mojalefa?' she asked, suddenly remembering that it might be years before she could speak to him like that again. She adored him, and speaking of parting with him broke her heart.

'I do not know, and I do not worry about that, Bongi. If I had you and Gugu and they thrust me into a desert for a thousand years, I would not care. But then I am only a small part of a whole. I'm like a single minute cell in the living body composed of millions of cells, and I have to play my small part for the well-being and perpetuation of life in the whole body.'

'But you are likely to be thrust into the midst of hardened criminals, murderers, rapists and so on.'

'Very likely. But then that should not deter us. After all most of them have been driven into being like that by the very evils we are exposed to as people without a say in the running of our lives. Most of them have ceased to be proud because there's nothing to be proud of. You amuse me, Bongi. So you think because we are more educated we have reason to be proud? Of what should we feel proud in a society where the mere

pigmentation of your skin condemns you to nothingness? Tell me, of what?'

She shook her head violently, biting her lips in
sorrow, and with tears in her eyes, she replied, softly,
'I do not know, Mojalefa.'

They stood in silence for a while. She sighed deeply and
held back the tears. They felt uneasy. It was useless,
she thought bitterly. They had gone through with what
she considered to be an ill-fated undertaking. Yet he
was relentlessly adamant. She remembered how they
had quarrelled the previous night. How at first she had
told herself that she had come to accept what was about
to happen with quiet composure, 'like a mature person'
as they say. She had however lost control of herself
when they were alone outside her home, when he had
bidden her mother and other relatives farewell. She had
become hysterical and could not go on pretending any
longer. In a fit of anger, she had accused Mojalefa of
being a coward who was running away from his
responsibilities as a father and husband. It had been a
very bad row and they had parted unceremoniously.
She had resolved that today she would only speak of
those things which would not make them unhappy. And
now she realised with regret that she was right back
where she had started. She murmured to herself, 'Oh
God, why should it be us, why should we be the lambs
for the slaughter? Why should you be one of those
handing themselves over? It's like giving up. What will
you be able to do for your people in gaol, or if you
should be . . .'

She could not utter the word 'killed'.

'*Somebody* has got to sacrifice so that others may be
free. The *real* things, those that really matter, are never
acquired the easy way. All the peoples of this world

who were oppressed like us have had to give up *some-thing*, Bongi. Nothing good or of real value comes easily. Our freedom will never be handed over to us on a silver platter. In our movement, we labour under no illusions; we know we can expect no hand-outs. We know that the path ahead of us is not lined with soft velvety flower petals: we are aware that we shall have to tread on thorns. We are committed to a life of service, sacrifice and suffering. Oh no, Bongi, you have got it all wrong. It is not like throwing in the towel. On the contrary, it is the beginning of something our people will never look back at with shame. We shall never regret what we are about to do, and there is no turning back. We are at the point of no return! If I changed my mind now and went back home and sat down and deceived myself that all was all right, I would die a very unhappy man indeed. I would die in dishonour.' He was silent a while.

'Bongi, I want to tell you my story. I've never related it to anyone before because just *thinking* about the sad event is to me a very unpleasant and extremely exacting experience. . . .' He was picking his way carefully through memories.

'After my father had completed altering that house we live in from a four-roomed match-box to what it is now, he was a proud man. He was called to the office by the superintendent to complete a contract with an electrical contractor. It had been a costly business and the contractor had insisted that the final arrangements be concluded before the City Council official. It was on that very day that the superintendent asked him if he could bring some of his colleagues to see the house when it was completed. My father agreed. I was there on that day when they (a group of about fifteen whites) arrived. I had heard my parents speak with great expectation to their friends and everybody about the intended "visit" by the white people. Naturally, I was delighted and proud as any youngster would be. I made sure I would be home and not at the football grounds that afternoon. I thought it was a great honour to have such respectable white people coming to *our* house. I looked forward to it and I had actually warned some of my friends . . .

'After showing them through all the nine rooms of the double-storey house, my obviously gratified parents both saw the party out along the slasto pathway to the front gate. I was standing with one of my friends near the front verandah. I still remember vividly the superintendent's last words. He said, "John, on behalf of my colleagues here and myself, we are very thankful that you and your kind *mosade* allowed us to come and see your beautiful house. You must have spent a *lot* of money to build and furnish it *so* well. But, *you should have built it on wheels!*' And the official added, with his arms swinging forward like someone pushing some imaginary object, "It should have had *wheels* so that it may *move* easily!" And they departed, leaving my petrified parents standing there agape and looking at each other in helpless amazement. I remember, later, my mother trying her best to put my stunned father at ease, saying, "Ao, o a blanya, mo lebale; ba a tsebe bore ontse a re'ng. Ntateble!" (He is mad; just forget about him. He does not know what he is saying!)

'As a fifteen-year-old youth, I was also puzzled. But unlike my parents, I did not sit down and forget – or try to do so. That day marked the turning point in my life. From that day on, I could not rest. Those remarks by that government official kept ringing in my mind. I had to know why he had said that. I probed, and probed; I asked my teachers at school, clerks at the municipal offices, anyone who I thought would be in a position to help me. Of course I made it as general as I could and I grew more and more restless. I went to libraries and read all the available literature I could find on the South African blacks.

'I studied South African history as I had never done before. The history of the discovery of gold, diamonds and other minerals in this land, and the growth of the towns. I read of the rush to the main industrial centres and the influx of the Africans into them, following their early reluctance, and sometimes refusal, to work there, and the subsequent laws which necessitated their coming like the vagrancy laws and the pass laws. I read about the removals of the so-called "black spots" and why they were now labelled that. The influenza epidemic which resulted in the building of the Western Native and George Goch townships in 1919. I dug into any information I could get about the history of the urban Africans. I discovered the slyness, hypocrisy, dishonesty and greed of the law-makers.

'When elderly people came to visit us and sat in the evenings to speak about their experiences of the past, of how they first came into contact with the whites, their lives with the Boers on the farms and so forth, I listened. Whenever my father's relations went to the remote areas in Lesotho and Matatiele, or to Zululand and Natal where my mother's people are, during school holidays, I grabbed the opportunity and accompanied them. Learning history ceased to be the usual matter of committing to memory a whole lot of intangible facts from some obscure detached past. It became a living thing and a challenge. I was in search of my true self. And like Moses in the Bible, I was disillusioned. Instead of having been raised like the slave I am, I had been nurtured like a prince, clothed in a fine white linen loincloth and girdle when I should have been wrapped in the rough woven clothing of my kind.

'When I had come to know most of the facts, when I had read through most of the numerous laws pertaining to the urban blacks – the acts, clauses, sub-clauses, regulations, sections and sub-sections; the amendments and sub-amendments – I saw myself for the first time. I was a prince, descended from the noble proud house of Monaheng – the true Kings of the Basuto nation. I stopped going to the sports clubs and the church. Even my father's flashy American "Impala" ceased to bring to me the thrill it used to when I drove round the townships in it. I attended political meetings because there, at least, I found people trying to find ways and means of solving and overcoming our prob-lems. At least I knew now what I really was . . . an underdog, a voiceless creature. Unlike my father, I was not going to be blindfolded and led along a garden path by someone else, a foreigner from other continents. I learnt that as a black, there was a responsibility I was carrying on my shoulders as a son of this soil. I realised that I had to take an active part in deciding (or in insisting that I should decide) the path along which my descendants will tread. Something was wrong: radically wrong, and it was my duty as a black person to try and put it right. To free myself and my people became an obsession, a dedication.

'I sometimes listen with interest when my father complains. Poor father. He would say: "Mojalefa *o a polotika*. All Mojalefa reads is politics, politics, politics. He no longer plays football like other youths. When he passed matric with flying colours in History, his History master came to my house to tell me how my son is a promising leader. I was proud and I moved around with my head in the air. I wanted him to start immediately at University, but he insisted that he wanted to work. I wondered why because I could afford it and there was no pressing need for him to work. He said he would study under UNISA* and I paid fees for the first year, and they sent him lectures. But instead of studying, he locks himself up in his room and reads politics all the time. He has stopped sending in scripts for correction. He is morose and never goes to church. He does not appreciate what I do for him!" Sometimes I actually pity my father. He would say, "My father was proud when Mojalefa was born. He walked on foot rather than take a bus all the way from Eastern Native Township to Bridgman Memorial Hospital in Brixton to offer his blessings at the bedside of my late wife, and to thank our ancestors for a son and heir. He named him Mojalefa. And now that boy is about to sacrifice himself – for what he calls 'a worthy cause'. He gives up all this . . . a' house I've built and furnished for R21,000, most of my money from the insurance policy my good old boss was clever enough to force me to take when I first started working for him. Mojalefa gives up all this for a gaol cell!" '

There were tears in the eyes of S'bongile as she sat staring in bewilderment at Mojalefa. She saw now a different man; a man with convictions and ideals; who was not going to be shaken from his beliefs, come what may. He stopped for a while and paused. All the time he spoke as if to some unseen being, as if he was unconscious of her presence. He went on, 'My father always speaks of how his grandfather used to tell him that as a boy in what is now known as the Free State (I don't know why) the white people (the Boers) used to come,

---

* The University of South Africa which teaches entirely by Correspondence.

clothed only in a "stertriem", and ask for permission to settle on their land. Just like that, bare-footed and with cracked soles, begging for land. My father does not realise that *he* is now in a worse position than those Boers; that all that makes a man has been stripped from under his feet. That he now has to *float in the air*. He sits back in his favourite comfortable armchair in his living-room, looks around him at the splendour surrounding him, and sadly asks, "When I go, who'll take over from me?" He thinks he is still a man, you know. He never stops to ask himself, "Take *what* over . . . a house on wheels? Something with no firm ground to stand on?" ' He turned away from her and looked through the dusty window pane. He raised his arms and grabbed the vertical steel bars over the window. He clung viciously to them and shook them until they rattled. He said, 'No Bongi. There is no turning back. Something has *got* to be done . . . something. It cannot go on like this!'

Strange as it may seem, at that moment, they both had visions of a gaol cell. They both felt like trapped animals. He kept on shaking the bars and shouting, 'Something's *got* to be done . . . Now!'

She could not bear the sight any longer. He seemed to be going through great emotional torture. She shouted, 'Mojalefa!'

He swung round and faced her like someone only waking up from a bad dream. He stared through the open entrance, and up at the stair leading to the upper floor where the humming voices were audible. They both stood still listening for a while. Then he spoke softly yet earnestly, clenching his fists and looking up towards the sound of the music. He said, 'Tomorrow, when dawn breaks, we shall march . . . Our men will advance from different parts of the Republic of South

Africa. They will leave their pass-books behind and not feel the heavy weight in their pockets as they proceed towards the gates of the prisons of this land of our forefathers!'

Bongi stood up slowly. She did not utter a word. There seemed to be nothing to say. She seemed to be drained of all feeling. She felt blank. He thought he detected an air of resignation, a look of calmness in her manner as she moved slowly in the direction of the opening into the street. They stopped and looked at each other. She sighed, and there were no tears in her eyes now. He brushed the back of his hand tenderly over the soft cheeks of the sleeping Gugu and with his dry lips, kissed S'bongile's brow. He lifted her chin slightly with his forefinger and looked into her eyes. They seemed to smile at him. They parted.

'Masechaba's Erring 'Child'

The houses in Orlando Extension all looked alike, especially when one was a stranger. They seemed to be so much bigger too. To one like Tholoana who lived in the 'normal' four-roomed match-box structure in Mapetla Extension, houses with bathrooms like the ones in Zwane Street were like palaces!

Tholoana tried to make out which one of the two adjacent houses with garages added on to the left-hand walls belonged to 'Masechaba. They looked *so* identical. Not that they were strikingly different from the other five-roomed houses in that area or in the whole of Orlando West Extension, no. They were in fact like loaves of bread which were baked in the same oven by an expert baker who had to turn out many hundreds of dozens of them before the break of another day. They were like the piping-hot loaves she and her work-mates at Mono Bakery in Fordsburg used to wrap in plastic bags until their shoulder-joints felt like they would snap out of their sockets and their wrists would ache long long after they had completed the tiresome task.

It was while serving the early-morning customers behind the glass counter of Mono that she got to know the owner of the 'big' house at Orlando Extension – the one she was now looking for. She remembered him now clearly as he had looked on that day when he walked into the bakery, going past the other two girls and a black man, all shop-assistants waiting along the counter to serve anyone who entered. He had walked right up to her, smiling and saying:, 'I want to be served by *this* young lady here.'

'Masechaba was bored and tired on that day. She had been handing over loaves of bread, packets containing cakes, tarts, scones, etc. to one customer after another, wearing (as usual) the 'forced' smile on her face, like the make-up and the ear-rings she had to adorn herself with every morning.

'I always want to be served by *you*,' the burly handsome well-dressed man repeated, emphasising the 'you' like he was addressing some distinguished lady and not just one of the many shop-assistants at Mono. This had taken Tholoana by surprise and she had asked, 'Why me?' to which the gentleman replied, 'Because you have dimples on your cheeks like my sister Nthati, and your ebony complexion is like the grain of beautiful brown cereal.'

Senatla was smiling; leaning slightly over the glass casement and whispering flirtatiously, his eyes exuding all the charm a man could employ. With the fourth finger of his left hand (round which he wore a shimmering signet ring) he kept brushing his thin thread-like moustache with the self-confidence of a man who was not without means.

Tholoana smiled now, picturing Senatla as he walked away in the direction of the white cashier to pay for his two loaves of bread which she had handed him, still taken aback by the gentleman's remarks. He gave her one final amorous look before stepping out of the entrance, swinging the keys of his latest brand new Biscayne which he had parked next to the pavement outside. He had ignored completely the giggling amused assistants who also turned to look at her standing there blushing and embarrassed.

The whole incident had taken Tholoana by surprise. Prior to that day, she had never even noticed Senatla . . .

'It *must* be the one with the high barbed-wire fence all around it,' Tholoana said to herself. It had been a long time since she had been to the house and *so* much had happened since then.

She had sworn, on that last occasion, that she would have nothing to do with the couple after he had cunningly enticed her to come to the house 'because', as he had explained, ''Masechaba is very ill, Tholoana. She has insisted that I should please bring you along with me. She has a very urgent message for you.'

She stood facing the silver-painted gate.

Tholoana remembered then how Senatla had used his own keys to unlock that same gate, locking it again carefully after he had let her in, and parked his car in the driveway. Yes, she thought, it was the one with the black wrought-iron numbers nailed on to the glazed wooden door.

She recalled that she had wondered why, in broad daylight, the gate had been locked securely when the 'ailing' 'Masechaba might need help and someone would have to come to the house.

But . . . she hesitated . . . the dog; the big alsatian dog. . . . Where was it? She remembered how she had stood dead-still halfway towards the door, totally shocked and trembling, expecting it to come charging at her. The dog had suddenly emerged from behind the short concrete terrace with the row of vases containing the evergreen shrubs and ferns that he personally tended and nurtured like an expert horticulturist. Realising her fright for the dog, he had chuckled re-assuringly, 'Please do walk in; don't worry. She won't bite you. She is so intelligent; she can smell out a friend from a foe like a "sangoma" can do.'

Tholoana remembered then how confident she had felt, and had entered the house only to find that 'Masechaba was not there.

It was six years before that and nearly nine-and-a-half months since Senatla had died of diabetes and hypertension.

The alsatian. . . . She stopped uncertainly at the gate not knowing what to do. Unlike the day she had been with Senatla, on that last decisive day, there was no padlock hanging on the gate. She could just push the gate and enter, but she was reluctant. Just as she was about to bend and pick up a small stone to throw it over the corrugated iron roof to 'announce' her presence at the gate, the lace curtains on the window to the right parted slightly and she could see 'Masechaba's smiling face peering through the opening. Tholoana felt happy. It had been a long time since she had last seen the kindly lady with her ever-smiling countenance, who she had come to like and admire so much.

But when 'Masechaba opened the door, and she observed the customary pitch-black worn apparel, her heart missed a beat. The reality of Senatla's death had, until then, only been some abstract vague occurrence which she had accepted without full realisation of what it would mean to the 'big' house in Zwane Street and its sole inhabitant, 'Masechaba.

It seemed ages since the news of Senatla's death had reached her. She was then in Pietermaritzberg where she was at the time nursing her aunt. In a letter to

Tholoana, Lindiwe, her best friend, had added simply a postscript to the letter: '. . . Oh, Tholo my dear, I nearly forgot. . . . U-"Biscayne" akasekho! I understand he was buried last Saturday. Thokozile, who you remember, came to work at Mono shortly before we left that place, met me in the train the other day and informed me. She attended the same church with the Senatlas in Phefeni.' The concise allusion to the sad episode had then only revoked in Tholoana's mind the memory of a nasty experience which had made her resent the very mention of 'u-Biscayne' – as the girls at Mono Bakery had come to nickname Senatla. But now, on this occasion, Tholoana no longer felt resentment but a deep feeling of compassion, especially when she thought what it must mean to 'Masechaba. There had never been any doubt in her mind that the dear lady really loved her husband.

Tholoana had sighed and whispered furtively, 'May God forgive him,' folding the letter thoughtfully, and putting it away. She and Lindiwe were now working as salesladies for Plastiware, a company selling plastic kitchen utensils and tableware. They were still very close friends like they had been at Mono. In fact, on this particular day, the two had been working as a team, going from house to house in the vicinity of the Senatla home. They had both agreed that it would be a good thing to pop in at the house and pay their respects to the dear bereaved lady. In such matters, it was never too late, they both agreed. As we say in our venacular: 'Motsilisi ha a nkuoe ke noka' (literal translation: One who brings his or her condolence is never drowned, i.e. It is never too late to console the bereaved). After all they had known the lady from Fordsburg where she had been working as a machinist at a nearby clothing factory.

'What a surprise Tholo! I'm really happy to see you. I always wanted to come to your home and let you and your dear mother know about . . . well, of course you must surely have heard by now . . .'

The widowed woman was smiling broadly as usual. She was standing at the threshold, her arms stretched out, waiting to receive Tholoana. At the entrance of the dining-room-cum-sitting-room, the two women were soon locked in a warm embrace.

Tholoana, looking over the older woman's shoulder, observed that the tidy polished pieces of dining-room furniture were arranged in exactly the same manner in which they had been the last time she was there, so long ago. As she sank into the thick cushioned floral sofa and looked at her own reflection in the mirror at the rear of the imbuia display cabinet, she could swear that nothing had been disturbed. Everything had been left exactly where it hàd been on that day. She even imagined that she could still remember the gleaming cut-glass water sets, the blue and white dinner-set, and the stainl-ess-steel tea-set occupying the very positions in which they had been then. The crockery, the cutlery-set in the maroon velvet case; the miniature brass and silver horses and carriages; the copper elephants, porcupines, cows and pigs; the wooden crocodiles, tortoises, camels, donkeys and giraffes – all were still there. Birds of every description – owls, peacocks, ostriches, doves, etc., all carved from horns of animals – black horns, white horns, grey horns – they were all still standing there, at the same spots as if they were nailed on to the shiny glass surface.

The shaggy carpet over which the legs of the heavy mahogany dining-room table straddled was still there covering the greater portion of the room, and, as if by design, 'allowing' the beholder to admire the zig-zag pattern of the plastic-coated wooden blocks over the entire floor space, giving the room the feeling of warmth and comfort.

'You're as beautiful as ever, Tholo. I'm *so* glad to see you again after such a long time! How are you, my dear?'

'Masechaba's voice sounded as if it came from the lips of a person far away. Stepping into that room had brought Tholoana 'face to face' with the shadow or image of a man she wanted to forget. While she was very happy to see 'Masechaba, the emotional conflict the image had evoked in her prevented her from expressing openly and freely her delight in being once more in the company of the older woman whom she had come to love and respect like her own sister. Their attraction for each other had become mutual, sincere and intense. Tholoana looked around, unable to shake off the imposing 'familiar' feel of the surroundings. She remarked, 'This room. . . . Everything is still as it was, 'Masechaba, just where it used to be . . . except the dog. What was the dog's name?'

'Jojo, you mean? I now keep it at the back of the house. It scares people. Late Sam, Ntate, nearly always left it free to make certain no one came in. He was such a careful person, always thinking of his property. Everything of his had to be where he wanted it. I miss him so much,' she said, holding back the tears which were already burning her eye-lids.

'I *did* hear about the sad death, 'Masechaba. I am really sorry that I could not be present at the funeral. I was in Pietermaritzburg at the time.'

'It was a big funeral we gave him. The church was packed full. As you know, he had been a person serving the people in church and as an agent for the African Burial Society. Many of the clients he had served so well in the East Rand, Brakpan, Benoni, Springs, Kwa-Thema, etc., they all came to pay their last respects. . . . But I missed you Tholo. In the last days when he was very ill and unable to get out of bed, he often inquired about you, you know. He never stopped to talk about you, my dear.'

'About me?'

'Yes, Tholo, about you. You were always a friend of ours. Surely you can't have forgotten that?'

'I . . . I . . . ,' Tholo stammered, resisting the urge to show her resentment and to deny the fact openly. She was thinking. While she respected and admired 'Masechaba very much, she was certainly not *his* friend. That reality had apparently not been appreciated by Senatla, who obviously mistook her frequent visits to 'Masechaba's home as a sure sign that she (Tholoana) really wanted to be near *him*. She remembered how silly Senatla used to look, trying hard to conceal his delight and excitement whenever she called. She tried to explain, 'I liked you very much and I still do admire you, 'Masechaba. If it had not been *you* insisting that I come often, I really do not think I would have been *his* friend. I'm sorry for speaking like that when Senatla is now . . . late . . . when he is no longer in this world, I mean, but . . .'

'I know, Tholo my dear. I know everything about you two. I know that . . . '

Just then, there was a voice calling from outside. The two women both started.

'Oh . . . ,' Tholo stood up to open the door, explaining, 'It must be Lindiwe. We were in this area doing demonstrations for the new firm we work for – Plastiware Home Pride – when I suddenly got the idea that we could call and see you. In fact I forgot to tell

145

you that we should expect someone in a car also looking for this place.'

Then, turning to Lindiwe who was already near the door, Tholoana remarked, 'That was quick. I thought you would take even longer than I to find the house Lindi. . . . Do come in dear.'

'The woman next-door where I was knew the Senatlas, so she directed me. It was easy,' Lindi said.

On seeing her, 'Masechaba exclaimed, Lindi too! This is surely a lucky day for me, I'm delighted. You too are just as radiant as when I last saw you at Mono. When did you two stop working there anyway? I see that you are driving now, Lindi. Is that your own car you parked there?'

'It must have been about six months after your factory (Dressy Creations) closed. We got tired of handling loaves of bread. As you can see, we now have better jobs.'

While she hugged 'Masechaba and took her seat, the three were now laughing loudly with Lindi boasting, 'It *is* my very own car, 'Masechaba my dear. Tholoana also has her own and she drives; only today we wanted to make it a combined effort. We give each other moral support and it does save petrol. Sometimes we use *her* car; hasn't she told you?'

'We were busy thinking of my dear husband. When one loses someone so close to her heart, it is easy not to avoid talking about it all the time,' the widow answered.

She then asked to be excused, adding, 'Surely this calls for a celebration, don't you two think that? I hope that you are in no hurry so that we can sit and talk about things. I'll try to hurry to the shops and get some biscuits. There was always excitement in this home whenever Tholo dropped in. I am not going to start changing things, not *that* part of life here. I'm so happy . . . !'

The two were left alone as 'Masechaba disappeared into the passage into the kitchen, and they could hear her speaking to Jojo outside, apparently 'telling' the dog that 'our big friend is here today'. They were looking around, with Tholo's mind still dwelling on the last time she was in that room. She whispered to her friend: 'You know, Lindi, why I delayed so long coming here to see 'Masechaba and console her, was really because I hated setting my foot inside this room. And now I am seeing everything just as it was on that day. I do not know why she has kept this place like this so long instead of rearranging the furniture. Surely she must be bored of seeing this same setting all the time. She tells me that she wants to keep everything "just as Ntate wanted it" as she puts it. I think it would be beneficial to her to stop going on as if Senatla was still here. After all *he* would have forgotten her the next minute after leaving her coffin at the cemetery. . . . I do not doubt that. You remember how he used to come again and again begging me to go with him in his Biscayne.'

'Yes, but ultimately he stopped, Tholo. He must have realised his unfaithfulness was not paying him.'

'It was not that at all. It was because I rebuffed him and said things to him that he did not expect. I can now remember everything so clearly like it happened only yesterday. I never told you the ghastly details. . . . He was so taken aback that he must have gone elsewhere to try is luck. I wanted to show him just how ridiculous he was; I said: "I came to your house only because I came to know your wife and like her. I know that she is a very wonderful person. She has taught me so many things - baking bread, wedding cakes, knitting and sewing. She is so good at handcraft that she is a real gem. I often asked her why she does not join women's organisations and teach other women how to do some of these things. Through what I learnt from her, I have been able to serve as an organiser and trainer at our local Self-help Club. She told me sadly one day that she had always wanted to own a dress-making business one day. She said that when you got married to her you promised her that you would even assist her. But after the marriage you told her that her place was in the home and not outside. All you were satisfied about, was to take her to work by car, drop her at the entrance of the factory, and collect her from there yourself every afternoon. You are cruel to your wife." When I said that, he was obviously offended and furious. He was also surprised because he never thought 'Masechaba could ever reveal so much of her suppressed feelings to anyone. He tried to argue, accusing me, "You're a liar! 'Masechaba is too decent a woman to go about saying things that are not true about her husband. She is a good woman. Besides, what happens between us is our business. She's very happy with how we live. She could never say or do anything behind my back!" I asked him, "So you want me to be unfaithful to the father of my child; you want me to do things behind his back?" And then he said something I would never forgive him for. He sneered, "So you refuse to go with me in my car even when I beg you because of that boyfriend of yours? OK I know he is known to be some kind of a leader and that many people admire him for what they say is 'his courage as an organiser and fighter for rights'. I know that his name is always in the papers and all that. . . ." I challenged him, "He is not a fighter for rights as you say. He is a fighter for *your* liberation. You speak as if what he is doing is just nonsense." Then he made me even more angry. He bellowed, "You're

only a single woman. You *need* a man. If we, married
men, never come to keep you company and take you
out, what would you do? You'd sit and wait for some
struggling 'tsotsi' to come along and take you to the
bioscope when he has stabbed someone and robbed him
on the packed trains? The divorcees, widows, spinsters
– they're all happy to meet men like me to carry them in
posh cars. . . . What makes you think you're different?
Wake up, girl, wake up!"

'When I took my bag and wanted to go, he would
not open the door. I told him that if he thinks that
women were created for *him* to play around with, then
he must think he is the Almighty. I said he can go to
women who are waiting for him to do them a favour
like he said, not *me*. He would not open the door. He
thought if he softened and begged me I would relent.
He pleaded, "Look. . . . Let's not fight, Tholo, please.
Let's enjoy ourselves. I took 'Masechaba to the farms
so that *you* may get a chance to be with me, please. Just
this once, please." He came towards me and I pushed
him away . . . against that display cabinet and I was
sure he would crash into it. He staggered, you see. I
did something he did not anticipate. He came towards
me again mumbling, bitterly, "No bloody single woman
has ever done this to me; not *me* . . . *I hope he dies in
gaol! I hope the Boers castrate him and strangle him!*"
I grabbed the vase from the table and flung it into his
face. . . . His eyes bulged out like balloons. He did not
think I would be brave enough to do that. His words
had provoked me and I no longer cared what happened.
I yelled at him: "*Coward* . . . Don't touch me! You sit
driving your posh cars to entice women and speak ill of
our heroes; people who are sacrificing their lives to free
you from bondage; coward, coward!" He was standing
there, dazed.

'Then I got the chance to unlock the door and bolt out. Near the gate the dog came charging at me. Up to this day, I do not know how I managed to remember what my father once said about most dogs retreating when you pretend to pick up a stone or something. It stood there snarling noisily as I screamed and people opposite there on the other side of the street stopped and looked on. He was forced to come out and open the gate. People knew him to be a respectable church-goer you know. . . . I never saw him again and I never told 'Masechaba.'

'I'm not surprised you rebuffed him like that. It must have been a very terrible experience, Tholo. You never spoke about it.'

They sat there looking at each other. The sound of approaching footsteps and 'Masechaba's voice humming a song happily were audible. Within minutes, their hostess entered with a tray and was ready to serve tea and biscuits. She was smiling as she passed the cups and 'reprimanded' Tholoana, 'I'm very happy you two are here, but I must say you've been cruel to me. The next time you come, please do warn me Tholo. I'll make it a point to bake you a cake myself. I won't go and buy old biscuits from the shops. You know very well that you are a special visitor in this house. By the way, I do not think that I have to be afraid to talk in Lindi's presence. I know that you two are bosom friends and that you do not keep anything from each other. Just before you came in, Lindi, I was telling Tholo that I knew everything about her and Ntate Sam. . . . Don't be uneasy Tholo my dear, I can see that you did not know that I knew everything.'

'Masechaba had in fact analysed Tholo's reluctance correctly. She had never suspected that Senatla could have confessed and revealed all that had happened between them to his wife. She was still not sure how to react to what 'Masechaba had said when she asked, 'What do you mean 'Masechaba? You don't mean to tell me that . . . '

'Yes, yes, I know everything, my dear,' she chipped in smiling. 'I even know that you refused him. . . . How could you be so cruel anyway? Ntate loved you so much. . . . He was nearly sobbing like a child when he told me. I couldn't help feeling very sorry for him.'

The two girls stared at 'Masechaba, astounded by what she was saying. Lindiwe managed to find her breath to say something. She asked, 'You really don't mean that you would have been happy to have the two . . . well . . . get along together when you were fully aware of it and you would not care, do you?'

'Of course I did not mind at all. I know Tholoana very well, I think. She is not the kind of woman who would snatch Sam from me, no; that much I know, Lindi. That is one of the reasons I really did not mind. Isn't it better to know everything your man is doing than to sit waiting for him to come home and he just goes for days or goes about dodging and bringing with him a whole lot of lies? I think *that* would just kill me. *I* certainly do not want to die slowly of heart failure like most women who never know what their husbands are about; who suffer, tearing themselves to pieces and suffering knowing and feeling that something must be wrong.'

Tholoana sat listening to the two, still too stunned to believe what she was hearing. 'Masechaba struck her as a completely different person from the shy, withdrawing shadow of a man who seemed to be sole master in the house, even over his wife's thoughts. With that 'Masechaba she knew, it was always 'Ntate o itse; Ntate o batla tjena; Ntate ha a batle hona, o batla hoane' all

151

the time that she got to know her. (Father said this; father wants this; father does not approve of this, he would rather have it done that way.) She was relieved that Lindi was there to ask questions she herself would have asked if she could summon courage to do so. She held her breath listening, looking from the one to the other. Lindi pursued her stand.

'I'm really puzzled. *I* would never just be satisfied to sit back and wait for a husband who is interested in going out with other women and leaving me at home all alone. . . . Oh now I see. It must be because you are a Southern Sotho. But most Basotho do not practise that tradition of accepting the husband's (or the wife's) lover any more. My own husband is a Mosotho but my goodness, he would rather die than put up with another man having access to me. I suppose Senatla didn't mind you going out with another man then, did he?'

'That would have been the last thing even to think of.'

'So? . . . *You* were satisfied with that kind of arrangement, one-sided as it was? Well, if the whole thing were to be fifty-fifty then *perhaps* one would tolerate it. If he can take a young woman and go out with her, then I must also be free to take a young man and do the same. *That* at least would be fair. Don't the Basotho traditional people do it that way?'

'You do not understand, Lindi. The whole thing would not work because in the home, let me say, in marriage, it is the husband's wishes which are important, not the woman's. If it makes him happy to "befriend" another woman, and that association is not going to disturb the marriage, then let him go ahead. The Basotho tradition has nothing to do with this. With these men of ours now, that is totally unacceptable. But what's the use of being stubborn and not letting him satisfy himself? It's useless because he will go about making love to other women anyway, whether you like it or not. What's the use of him sitting with you, being bored because his heart is elsewhere? I have seen many men bury their faces in books and newspapers because they no longer speak to their wives and they do not enjoy their company. What's the use of that?'

'Then in that case he no longer *wants* his wife. If he would rather be with another woman to be happy then why stay with his wife?'

'But if you allow him to make himself happy the way he wants, then he will come home feeling good and you won't have to put up with a difficult morose person next to you who cannot even smile with you any more. What do you think would happen if he went about with people you do not know? He would perhaps even take your money and go and spend it with those women and you would not be able to have anything in the house.'

'I would not give him the money then if he misuses it that way.'

'But how would you know? It's better if he tells you everything so that you can also make your demands. Senatla used to make sure my refrigerator is full of meat and other things that I need. He also used to go with me to the clothing shops and I would choose whatever I wanted and he would pay, and of course I knew that he also banked what was left. He used to satisfy me with what I wanted and then tell me that he will be going with whoever he was going out with. The trouble with these irresponsible single women is that they always want to *take a man and keep him*. That I cannot have. The man must always know that he must come back to *me*.'

'Then you are just as good as his grandmother. Come back to you to do what, smile and ask you to wash his shirts and iron his trousers so that he is spic and span when he goes to the other woman? That would be the day!'

'Do you mean to tell me that you want to sit and fret, while some woman somewhere (who perhaps even knows you) is laughing privately and making a fool out of you while you talk and smile with her when she is "eating your heels" ("a u ja lirethe")? I would rather know her, my dear sister.'

'I would only want to tear her to pieces every time I met her. I would never stand the sight of her. The fact that a man leaves me with a fridge full of meat or not has nothing to do with our life as husband and wife. It is not the meat I married, but *him*.'

'If you did not know what your husband is doing when he is not with you, you would always be insecure. You would imagine all sorts of things. I have seen men who are infatuated with other women leave their wives or drive them out when they did not even suspect that they were having affairs. What a nasty experience it is when you suddenly see your husband walk in one day all sulky and not smiling, telling you from nowhere, "Lindi, just pack your clothes and leave, I have found someone else"? I have actually seen women go crazy because of the shock of being driven out by husbands they never knew could *look* at another woman. Have you not met such women?'

'Yes there are such cases I know, but still for all, a woman is also a person. She can refuse to go.'

'How can she refuse when she is already mad and fit for Sterkfontein Mental Hospital? I don't want to go about "eating grass" as we say. I must know what is happening. I knew and approved of Tholo, for instance, because I could see that she is a hard-working and serious young lady who was also proud of herself and not just one of these smiling snaky man-snatchers. I do not want to lose everything I have slaved for in my house just because my husband is weak. Where should I go and look for another one? Most of them *are* like that anyway. How many lovely self-respecting women have been dumped by their husbands just because the man cannot resist the smile of a silly hussy? *My* sweat is not going to be "eaten" by any passing petticoat, no! No little smiling beauty who has never done a stitch of work in her life but chase "hungry" men around with the hope of floating easily into comfort which my husband and I have slaved side by side to create for ourselves and our children. No, Lindi; I have seen far too many children roaming the streets and picking up dirty orange peels because they and their mothers have been chucked right out of their homes. What do you think, Tholo, don't you think I'm right? You have not uttered a word since we started on this subject; why?'

'It is because you really surprise me 'Masechaba. I never knew that you could be so selfish. You only think of yourself.'

That statement was unexpected by both 'Masechaba and Lindi. The latter looked at her friend questioningly. She asked her, 'How could you think that? As far as *I* am concerned, 'Masechaba is far more willing to share than most women. If she does not mind offering her husband to other women like that then. . . .'

Tholo did not wait for Lindi to complete the sentence. She had by now become wholly involved and was so carried away by the arguments of the two women that she even felt impatient to speak. She snapped in, smiling into 'Masechaba's face: 'From what I gather, in this eagerness of yours to assist your husband, it would seem that you totally ignored the fact that *I* am a human being with feelings. All you wanted to do was to do everything in your power to get him what *he* wanted. Unfortunately this mere "object" which is to make your husband happy come what may, happened, in this case,to be *me*. I do not know what his *other* "friends" in whom he was interested from time to time would have felt like. Of course I would not speak for *them*. But for goodness' sake, what about *me* ? What was I to be in this case; a lamb to be sacrificed; a dumb thing? You never stopped to think about *my* feelings. You just thought that in my case, your husband would remain safely "near" you to maintain the image of a real husband and not leave you or drive you out of the house and deprive you of everything you had worked hard for. Did you ever consider that I might be having my own man whom I loved and wanted to stay faithful to? Even if that had not been the case, I might not necess- arily have wanted to play second fiddle to you. Surely I have my own pride?'

Lindi nodded, also smiling. She said, 'You know, Tholo, you are right. I wonder why I never gave it a thought. 'Masechaba was really selfish. She only wanted to use you to make her husband "easier to live with" as she suggested a while ago. So your husband could do anything as long as you were not "pushed" out of the house is it?' she asked, looking at their hostess.

'Of course, he kept the roof above my head, what could I do?' the older lady said, shrugging her shoulders helplessly.

Lindi concluded, 'Then you didn't love him. I would think a person does not even *like* me if he gave me so much licence. You didn't want to be chased out of the house, that's all. What about being chased out of his heart? I still think the heart is more important than the *house* in marriage!'

They all laughed. Tholo remarked, 'Honestly we are

laughing but this is a very serious matter. I really did
not know that *you* 'Masechaba, of all people, would not
care about me to that extent. I always thought I could
look upon you as my own sister; but now . . .'

'Of course I adore you, Tholo my dear. It was only
that I thought that you would be willing to . . .'

Tholo cut her short sharply: 'To do what; be
dishonest to my own boy-friend? Surely you knew that
I had a boy-friend and that I had a child by him, didn't
you?'

'Yes, I knew. But we never talked about him. I never
really knew him. Besides you never used to bring him
whenever you paid us a visit. All Sam used to say was
that he was some kind of a leader.'

'At the time, he was in gaol, detained for organising
protest marches. Surely you must have known that;
everybody read about him; didn't you?'

'Do what? Read papers? Why should I read papers?
Ntate was the one who read papers. In any case he
never said anything about what he read in the papers
and I only used them to make fire. There were too
many of them everywhere. There's *so* much work I have
to do in the house, why should I sit and read papers?'

The others shook their heads, looking at each other
and smiling. Then Tholoana remembered some of their
conversations. She asked, 'By the way, you have a property in Evaton. What happened to it, did you persuade
him to build you a house there like you said you were
trying? I remember you saying he is reluctant to build
you a house "because", as he put it, "as soon as you
have completed building a big house for a woman, you
are sure to die first and leave her enjoying the fruits of
your labour alone, or with other men," also that he
would add that "that is why in Sophiatown where he

grew up, there were many widows left behind on huge properties and virtually swimming in comfort"!'

By the time Tholo concluded the sentence, the three were already laughing loudly, with Lindi adding, 'Oh yes; I have heard that one before about Sophiatown having been a city of widows and that women are in the habit of murdering their husbands, shame.'

'Masechaba did not know anything about the Evaton property. She knew very little about the car. Yet she claimed that Senatla told her everything. She confessed, 'To tell the truth, I never bothered to ask about the property or the car because Ntate said that those were a man's business, not a woman's.'

Tholoana felt annoyed by 'Masechaba's child-like behaviour. Even the way she kept on calling Senatla 'Ntate' (Father), especially because she seemed to obey him – not as a loving companion, but as a daughter would do. She shook her head and said, 'Oh no, not at all. What you both work for is the business of both of you. So you were only good for working, and bringing in money; and not good enough to know what happens to that money afterwards.'

Lindiwe nodded, smiling sardonically. She added, 'So all you were really worried about was his relationship with other women and not property; possessions, which are so important. As far as I am concerned, the wife should make it her business to know everything, especially property, cars and so on. What if Senatla took your money and bought girls presents?'

'It seems to me that 'Masechaba was only satisfied to be carried around (when it was convenient for the "boss") from one place to another. What were you, a parcel – removed from point A and delivered to point B, my goodness! The car should be available to both of you so that both of you can use it when either of you feel like using it,' Lindi chipped in, looking at Tholoana.

'I bet Senatla did not even want 'Masechaba to learn how to drive,' the other agreed.

'Masechaba nodded shyly. 'Yes. He always used to say that I am "too soft" to drive. That since I am scared even of a small mouse, I would never be able even to sit behind the steering-wheel – let alone drive. He said driving was for tough people. Oh how I wish I could drive my own car like you two fortunate girls!'

Lindiwe replied, her eyes opened widely, looking at 'Masechaba, 'Frankly I do not know why you cannot drive if you can instruct all those women how to do all that wonderful baking and cooking at the club, even if you are afraid of a mouse. I know of very many men – fully grown men – who are scared to go near a new-born baby, let alone touch it. Even a small girl can bring up a baby, feed it, cuddle it and make it comfortable. All you were good for was washing for him, cooking for him and making him a nice-looking sugar-daddy.

'That would be the last thing for me to do. If I do all those things for him, then it must be because he loves me. If he prefers to rather clean the house than cook, then good. It would only be fair. Let him do the garden, plant flowers, tend the lawn, grow vegetables, mend broken cupboards, do the painting and so on. If I have to do everything, then he, too, must do everything. He must cook, wash, iron, bake, all that.'

By the time Lindiwe finished enumerating all those duties she said her husband would have to perform, 'Masechaba was already clapping her hands in dismay. She chuckled, her eyes pointed at the ceiling. 'Ao, Ao, Ao! Then you would be turning him into a woman. Everyone will say that you have given him "korobela" (a potion to make him timid and harmless). Ntate would never do all that. Even the gardening business, he would never do. He would rather get someone to do all that and pay him.'

Tholoana remarked 'So Senatla was the kind of man who would enslave one woman in order to pamper another woman, as long as she is not his wife. My man believes in the freedom of the individual, in trust and faith in the one you love. He does not believe in tying anyone in chains. That is why he'd rather go to gaol to fight this vicious system which manacles people. I often wonder whether he (Senatla) would like his mother or sister or aunt to be treated the way he treated women. I believe he was doing that to you because you are not his flesh and blood.'

'Masechaba seemed to be touched by all that was being said. She felt like she would be cruel and not respectful to the man she worshipped so much. She spoke softly in mediation. 'I allowed him to enjoy himself just like you allow a child to play. He was like a child – an erring child, that's all. I kept on hoping that he would one day grow up and stop his child-like ways but he never. I grew tired of trying, tired.'

'Oh men! Then they wonder why women wish them dead. No doubt you feel like a fully-grown person now that he is no longer around, eh?'

The two younger women pitied 'Masechaba. No doubt Senatla had become increasingly senile. What kind of a 'child' would go about seducing women and young girls? Many unanswered questions lingered in the minds of the two visitors. 'Masechaba was a lonely woman who obviously needed to be loved and helped through a difficult time. She insisted that the two should come on another day when they were not very busy to accompany her to Evaton. She was now determined to find out what was going on with the property. She felt certain that the tenants there would tell her about any outstanding rentals. It would be very helpful if she could get extra income. She desperately needed it.

On the appointed day, the three women drove to Evaton. From the tenants, they learnt that a certain man – a resident of the township – was paying monthly visits to the property to collect rent on behalf of a firm of lawyers in Johannesburg.

A visit to the offices of the lawyers shattered all 'Masechaba's hopes. The property she thought they still had had been sold by her husband to Messrs Symon & Symon Limited some five years prior to his death. She knew nothing of the whole transaction. Senatla had been paid fully for the property.

O ile a ikutloa a nyahame, a feletsoe ke matla 'me a se na tšepo: a fefoha joaleka ha e ka o tsukutliloe ke lifefo le maqhubu leetong la bophelo bona. She felt helpless and without strength; too drained of all energy – like a weightless, tempest-torn being – hurled hither and thither by strong winds and violent waves in this life's journey. She felt many more years older than her fifty. She was disillusioned and her spirits were broken. The truth stared at her in the face. The man she had trusted and worshipped had betrayed her. It had been a long, tiring and sad day. Before she alighted, she made a final request to the girls. 'Tholoana, and you Lindiwe, please *do* come and see me as soon as possible, after I have gone through the cleansing ceremony in two months' time. I would like you to arrange that I take driving lessons as soon as I can. And, thank you both for all that you have done for me.'

They watched her trudge slowly along the pathway leading from the gate to the house. At the door, she turned to wave her hand at her departing friends. She opened the door and stepped into the house.